AWAKENED
WITH PLEASURE...

When he awoke, Longarm found himself being led groggily into Mary's bedroom. She pushed him gently back onto the bed and proceeded to undress him. In a moment her corset was off, and she was wearing only her shift. As he gaped, she stepped out of the shift and smiled at him.

"You had a nice nap," she told him. "Now it's time for you to thank me proper for that meal—and for all the information I am going to give you."

She fell forward onto his broad chest and nipped his earlobe.

"You still hungry?" he asked, his weariness falling away instantly as he closed his arms about her.

"For you I am..."

TABOR EVANS

LONGARM

AND THE BIG OUTFIT

A JOVE BOOK

LONGARM AND THE BIG OUTFIT

A Jove Book / published by arrangement with
the author

PRINTING HISTORY
Jove edition / October 1983
Second printing / December 1983
Third printing / September 1984

ISBN: 0-515-07886-7

Jove books are published by The Berkley Publishing Group,
200 Madison Avenue, New York, N.Y. 10016.
The words "A JOVE BOOK" and the "J" with sunburst
are trademarks belonging to Jove Publications, Inc.

PRINTED IN THE UNITED STATES OF AMERICA.

LONGARM

AND THE BIG OUTFIT

Chapter 1

There was a grim, unhappy cast to his features as Deputy U.S. Marshal Custis Long strode swiftly up Colfax Avenue, heading for the gleaming dome of the Colorado State House. He had a painful announcement to make to his chief, Billy Vail. It had taken Longarm a long, sleepless night to come to his decision, and now that he had, he was hurrying so that nothing would be allowed to change his mind.

Still on the comfortable side of forty, the raw sun and cutting winds he'd ridden through since coming West from West-by-God-Virginia had cured Longarm's rawboned features to a saddle-leather brown. His eyes were gunmetal blue, set wide over high cheekbones. Only the tobacco-leaf shade of his close-cropped hair and longhorn mustache gave evidence of

Anglo-Saxon birth. Otherwise, to the casual observer, he could easily have passed for a full-blooded Indian.

He wore his snuff-brown Stetson dead center and tilted slightly forward, cavalry style—the hat's crown telescoped in the Colorado rider's fashion. Over his buttoned vest he wore a brown frock coat that matched his brown tweed pants.

The pants clung snugly to his lean frame. They had been purchased a size too small. Longarm knew the dangers of a sweat-soaked fold of cloth or leather between a rider and his mount moving far or sudden. His low-heeled cavalry stovepipes had been purchased a size too short for a similar reason. He had soaked them overnight and put them on wet to dry as they were broken in, molding themselves to his feet in the process. Longarm spent as much time on foot as he did astride a horse, and in these boots he could run with surprising speed for a man his size.

Under his frock coat, on his left side, he carried a Colt Model T .44-40 in a cross-draw rig fashioned of waxed and heat-hardened leather. This was not, however, the only piece of artillery he carried. In his right vest pocket, acting as a fob for his watch, he carried a double-barrelled .44 derringer. For a small gun it packed quite a wallop, and it had proven its worth in more than one encounter.

Reaching the federal courthouse, Longarm strode through the crowded first-floor lobby and climbed the marble staircase. He moved down a short hall to a door on which gold leaf lettering proclaimed: UNITED STATES MARSHAL, FIRST DISTRICT COURT OF COLORADO. Pushing through the door, he skirted a young clerk

2

pounding on one of those newfangled engines called typewriting machines, knocked once on Billy Vail's office door, and strode in.

"That's right," snarled Vail, glancing up momentarily from his paper-strewn desk. "Just walk right in, Longarm. Don't bother to knock. What the hell, I'm just your boss."

Longarm did not reply.

"Sit down," Vail told him gruffly. "I'll be with you in a minute. Some damned bureaucrat in Washington will pee in his pants if I don't get this off to him right now, today."

Instead of dropping his lean frame into Vail's moroccan leather armchair, as was his custom, Longarm remained standing as he watched his harried superior slaving over his paperwork. In his salad days Marshal Billy Vail had shot it out with Comanche, Owlhoots, and, to hear him tell it, half of Mexico. But now he was running to lard. Already his face had become a soft, almost babyish pink, as if old age were turning him back into an infant.

Longarm cleared his throat. Billy Vail glanced up and frowned.

"Sit down! Sit down, will you?"

"I'd rather not, Chief."

Frowning, Vail pushed himself away from his desk and looked more closely at Longarm. For the first time he noticed the grim, unsmiling cast to his deputy's face.

"Well, what is it this time, Longarm? You getting sick of the stink of Denver? All this coal smoke giving you asthma, is that it?"

"Billy," said Longarm, "I'm quitting."

It took a second or two for Vail to take it in. Then he jumped to his feet, bellowing, "You are *what?*" The banjo clock on the oak-paneled wall shook.

"You heard me, Billy."

"My God, Longarm! You aren't serious!"

"I've been thinking about it all night," his deputy replied.

"Well, go back and think about it for another night!"

"I mean it, Billy."

"Damn it, Longarm, you owe me an explanation!"

"I got business to tend to."

"Business?"

"Personal business."

"Then tend to it. I won't stop you. You know that."

"It'll take time, and I don't know how much. It's best I quit and go see to it."

"Are you going to tell me what this is all about?"

Longarm took out a telegram he had received the day before. "Here," he said. "Read this."

Vail took the telegram and slumped back into his chair. Longarm sat down also.

After reading it swiftly, Vail glanced up, frowning. "I think I remember Juan, don't I? Didn't he stop in here with you last fall?"

Longarm nodded.

"Of course. I remember now. The two of you are partners in a small ranch in the Tetons."

"I staked him to half the purchase price and he made me a full partner. I didn't argue. When I get tired of chasing no-accounts, I might want to settle down."

"Yes," Vail said, his eyes suddenly contemplative, "on a quiet little ranch in the Tetons. You told me about it once when you were drunk. You wanted me

4

to quit this job before I got too fat and join you, as I recall." Smiling some at the recollection, Vail handed the telegram back to Longarm. "I can understand your concern. Juan did not appear to me to be capable of murder."

Longarm folded the telegram and put it away. "He isn't. As the telegram says, he has been arrested for murder and might go to jail. It's a frame of some kind, I am sure of it."

"And you want to go up there to investigate."

"I know it's a long way from here, and I don't know how much time it will take. But I owe my life to Juan Romero, Billy. And now he's asking for my help."

"Then go."

"You saying I can go without quitting?"

"Ordinarily, there's no way I could allow it on government expense or government time. But you're in luck, Longarm. How does this sound to you? I'll send you to Moose Creek, where Wallace is still holding that train robber. He's recovering nicely from his wound, I understand, but he may need help, so I'm sending you there to give him any assistance he may require. As soon as Wallace is able to get himself and his prisoner safely on a train for Denver, you can start back." He winked broadly. "But take your time. See what I mean?"

"How much time?"

"A week, maybe."

"It'll take longer, I'm thinking."

"Then take longer—but not too damn long!"

Longarm blew his cheeks out and shook his head. "Maybe it'd be simpler if I just turned in my badge."

Vail ran his pudgy hand down over his face. "All right. Take as long as you need. I'll back you all the way. Damn it, Longarm, you got me over a barrel. I don't want to lose you. You're the best man I got."

Longarm took a deep breath and smiled for the first time since he had received the telegram. "Thanks, Chief. I appreciate it."

"You'd better." Vail grinned back at Longarm suddenly. "Get your gear ready and we'll get the expense vouchers and your railroad pass ready."

As Longarm pulled the door open, Vail cleared his throat. Pausing, the deputy looked back.

"Take care of yourself, you long-legged galoot. And give my regards to Juan."

"I will, Chief. Thanks."

The distant rattle of rifle fire sounded again.

Pulling his mount to a halt, Longarm lifted his head to listen. The ragged sound seemed to have shocked the mountainside around him into a waiting silence. The echoing roll of gunfire faded, then died away completely. Cursing softly and bitterly, Longarm urged his horse forward again up through the timber, his eyes probing the ridgeline above him. Despite his desire to make the ridge as quickly as possible, he refused to push his big horse into a gallop.

In the time it took him to gain the ridge, there was no resumption of the gunfire. But it gave Longarm little comfort as he followed along the crest of the ridge to a vaguely familiar trail leading down through a slim stand of jack pine on the far side.

Riding slack in the saddle to save his mount, Longarm cut down through the timber. His face was drawn with fatigue. He had wasted only two days with Wallace and then cut northwest into the Tetons, riding hard and fast for nearly a week, at times traveling on through moonlit nights, so anxious was he to talk to Juan—or his wife, in the event that Juan was still in jail awaiting trial.

But all during the ride, he had the nagging sense that he was going to be too late, or that the trouble was coming on too hard. And now that ominous rattle of gunfire indicated that his fears had not been groundless. Juan was in trouble—bad trouble.

Longarm emerged at last into a small clearing overlooking a lush valley watered by a swift mountain stream. The sun had already dipped below the ridgeline behind him, and the valley floor was in shadow. Longarm patted the neck of his mount to quiet him and peered down intently at the small cluster of ranch buildings that made up the J Bar Ranch.

The buildings were set close beside the stream, an icy, snow-fed torrent Longarm and Juan had fished several years ago, before Longarm had taken his job as a deputy U.S. marshal. The two men had been busy most of that long, beautiful summer building the log cabin, the lodgepole corrals, the pole-and-shake barn. But, in the light of a fading sun, the sight of the modest spread did not please Longarm.

There should have been sleek stock grazing in the lush pastures, horseflesh in the corrals. Longarm should have heard the sound of chickens scolding and scratching from within the barn. But, in fact, there was no sign of activity at all. Over the cabin, as over the entire valley, there hung an ominous, waiting silence.

Suddenly Juan's wife darted from the cabin and

headed for the stream, a wooden bucket in her hand. Longarm recognized Carlotta's long slender figure at once. One glance at the way she moved told Longarm she was in danger. Dismounting swiftly, he snaked his Winchester from its scabbard.

A rifle shot cracked from somewhere around the cabin, but the woman kept moving. The shot had obviously been meant to warn her, to send her back to the cabin. A small explosion at her feet showed how close the bullet had come. Another shot echoed, but the woman continued to walk calmly and impassively toward the stream. A third shot caught the wooden bucket in its side and tore it from Carlotta's grasp. Bounding away like something alive, it cleared the bank and plunged into the stream, sinking almost immediately.

Juan's wife looked around at her unseen tormentors and raised a defiant fist. Then she started back to the cabin. Another shot rang out, from someone who was obviously infuriated by her courage. This shot, however, had been cut too close. Carlotta staggered forward a few steps, then crumpled to the ground. There was a hoarse, angry cry from someone holed up near the barn, ordering the rest of the besiegers to hold their fire.

The firing ceased as those outside the cabin watched the wounded woman begin to crawl back to the cabin. At last she ceased crawling and again collapsed forward onto the ground. Longarm felt sick. Then, from within the cabin, came Juan's faint cry of anguish as he caught sight of Carlotta. The glint of Juan's revolver was visible for a moment in the doorway's dark rectangle, a second before he darted out of the cabin.

8

Grabbing Carlotta about the shoulders, Juan began to pull her back into the cabin.

But the sight of their quarry was too much for Juan's besiegers. They opened up once again. Longarm's rage turned to cold fury when he saw a bullet slam Juan back against the cabin wall. Still holding onto Carlotta, Juan managed somehow to pull her back inside.

The firing was a steady fusillade now as Longarm swiftly and silently descended the steep slope, his eyes searching the bushes and rocks below him. Before he reached the bottom, darkness had completely enveloped the valley.

Chapter 2

It was entirely dark by the time Longarm negotiated the shallow stream and drifted cat-like into the brush bordering it. A moment later, flat on his belly, he found himself moving up on one of the besiegers from behind.

The fellow was crouched behind the corral fence, his hat tipped back on his head, his rifle on the ground beside him. Longarm was almost to him when his foot caught a section of loose gravel. As the fellow started to turn, Longarm closed his finger about the trigger of his Winchester, prepared to fire.

"Hi, Billy," the man said casually, glancing back for an instant, then looking at the cabin once again. "I wish you'd go back and tell Sheriff Swenson we

11

should pull out. This is a miserable damn business."

Longarm lowered his Winchester and muttered something unintelligible as he slipped closer.

"I know this here post was Slim's last night," the young man went on unhappily, "and I guess it's only fair I should spell him tonight. But I'm getting a mite weary of this business. I purely am."

Almost beside the man now, Longarm made another meaningless grunt and pulled the brim of his hat down to keep his face in shadow. Glancing only briefly at Longarm, the fellow slumped with his back to a fence post. He seemed glad of the company. By this time it was so dark that Longarm could no longer make out the cabin doorway, even though they were less than twenty yards from it.

"Where's the horses?" Longarm asked, coughing at the same time to disguise his voice.

"Hell, Billy, you know where. Grazing by the cottonwoods in the flat. Labeau and Slim are taking care of them to see they don't spook from all this shooting. Why? You think of pulling out?"

Longarm shrugged.

"Well, I'd sure like to get back to June. Yes, I would. I been away from my woman too long. Too damn long." He swore softly and shook his head as he contemplated the pleasures he was missing holed up outside this cabin.

Longarm, so close to the besieger now that he could have reached out and strangled him if he wished, kept his back to him and peered through the corral at the cabin's dim shape. With the moon still out of sight behind the mountains, he had a chance to make it to the cabin and out again with Juan and Carlotta—if he

12

could get rid of this young posse member beside him without too much of a fuss.

"I think we done enough for Murchison and that damned outfit of his," the fellow went on irritably. "He's too darn big for its britches, I say. The Big Outfit, they call it." He sighed wearily. "Maybe they ought to call it the Pig Outfit. Seems to me, the bigger that spread gets, the greedier Murchison gets. I say three days holed up outside this cabin is enough, Big Outfit or no Big Outfit."

His back still to the fellow, Longarm uttered another unintelligible grunt. This seemed to be all the young fellow needed to continue.

"Yes sir, I got my belly full, I can tell you that," he droned on. "That was a goddamn turkey shoot back there a few minutes ago."

"You liked it?" Longarm asked, suddenly angry enough not to care if he gave himself away.

"Hell, no! You'd have to be a redskin to like that sort of thing!"

Longarm turned to face the young man. "Go on back to the sheriff and tell him, why don't you. Tell him to pull out."

Longarm saw the man's head swivel suddenly as he peered through the gloom. Watching him closely, Longarm realized at once that the fellow knew now that Longarm was not a fellow posse member—not Billy at all, but someone else.

"Sure, sure, Billy," the fellow said hastily, pulling away. "I'll go see Clint right now—tell him what you said."

Snatching up his rifle, he pulled swiftly back toward the creek. When he reached it he plunged in, and, keeping low, started wading upstream toward the barn. Longarm watched him closely, his Winchester's sights centered on the shadowy figure. He was determined to give the young fool a chance to get away, if he was smart enough to take it.

He wasn't. He whirled to fire on Longarm, his rifle barrel glinting as he swung it up. Throwing himself flat, his own Winchester out in front of him, Longarm fired first. The young man uttered a soft cry and vanished. Longarm heard him strike the water just as the rest of the posse, startled into action by Longarm's shot, resumed firing at the cabin.

Still flat on the ground, Longarm waited for the fusillade to ease up, noting where the flashes of gunfire were coming from, and their number. He counted four posse members in all. One was firing from behind the barn, another from the cottonwoods north of the cabin. Two others were firing from downstream. These two, Longarm figured, were Labeau and Slim, the two posse members who'd been assigned to wrangle the horses.

Longarm waited patiently as the lead whined overhead. In the darkness the posse could only have assumed that the shot they had heard had come from the young man guarding the cabin door, firing at some movement within the cabin—or that Juan had fired at the posse member.

Gradually, when no return fire came from the cabin, the posse's enthusiasm waned and they ceased throwing good lead after bad. After waiting a moment or two longer to make sure that the posse members were through firing, Longarm began to crawl across the open ground toward the cabin. He kept his head low and did not hurry. Any noise he made would alert

Juan—assuming he was not too badly wounded—and might cause him to begin shooting.

Less than a yard from the doorway, Longarm called out Juan's name. There was no answer. Longarm crept still closer and called again, more loudly.

This time Juan answered. His voice did not sound good. "Custis! You crazy son of a bitch! Get in here!"

Longarm was relieved to hear Juan's voice, and pulled himself the rest of the way into the cabin. As he did so, his left hand came down on Carlotta's dress. He caught her arm. It was cold. He pulled his hand away.

"Over here," Juan called softly. "In this corner."

The inside of the cabin was black as pitch, and the corner to which Juan directed Longarm was to his right. When he reached Juan's side, Longarm saw that Juan had poked a hole in the chinking between the logs, enabling him to see out across the yard as far as the steep-sided slopes of the mountainside on the other side of the stream. The blackness of the cabin's interior seemed to give an uncannily clear illumination to the moonless world outside.

Juan reached out and took Longarm's hand.

"Carlotta is dead, *amigo*," he told Longarm softly. "She is there by the door. They gave her a chance to leave earlier, but she would not go without me." Juan sighed in bitter anguish. "I pleaded with her to leave me. Then, not long ago, like a fool, I mentioned how thirsty I was—and she went out for water. I could not stop her. She would not listen. She said only, 'You are thirsty, so I will get water...' Son of a bitch, Custis! I should never have told her!"

Juan was sitting with his back to the wall, and in

the darkness Longarm could not be sure how severe his wounds were, but Juan's voice did not sound very strong.

"I saw the whole thing from the ridge, Juan. How bad are you hurt?"

"It is all right, Custis. I am not bleeding that much."

"Where were you hit?"

"The first time in the left arm. The second time—when I went after Carlotta—in the chest. The arm is broken. The other one sits like a branding iron under my left collarbone. This is the big one, *amigo.*"

By this time Longarm's eyes had adjusted enough to the darkness for him to be able to see Juan more clearly. Juan's already lean face was now gaunt, his eyes were like dark wounds, and he was obviously in great pain.

"I got your telegram late, Juan," Longarm explained, "but I came as fast as I could."

"You came, *amigo*. That is enough."

"The telegram said you were accused of murder. What happened? What's a posse doing outside here?"

"I got off. A good lawyer—and the judge, too. He is an honest man. But Pete Murchison would not let it go at that. He is convinced that I killed his son."

"How come?"

"They found his son on my land, dead. That was enough for Murchison."

"What was Murchison's son doing on your land?"

"If I knew that, I would have been able to help myself. But I know nothing—except that I did not do it."

"This Murchison—who is he?"

"The biggest man around. Owns the Double M. They call it the Big Outfit."

"And this Murchison is convinced you killed his son. But how does that suspicion tie in with that posse out there?"

"Murchison owns the sheriff, along with everything else around here. After the trial, when I was let go, Murchison told me he'd get me. He made no bones about it. No slick lawyer or crooked judge was going to prevent him from avenging the murder of his son. Not long after, someone hung a steer in my barn. And, of course, a Double M hand happened by and found it."

Longarm nodded grimly. The frame was simple and effective, and as transparent as spring ice. "So now they've come after you, to string you up for rustling."

"That's right, *amigo*. One way or another, Murchison is going to get me for killing his son."

Longarm shook his head in frustration. "I should have got here sooner."

"Do not blame yourself. Blame those bastards out there in that posse."

"Yes."

"Anyway, Custis, you came, and that is enough. Now it is like the old days, hey? Remember how it was that time before? You and me against that pack of miners?"

"I remember."

"Now all that is over. Soon I will join Carlotta."

"Don't talk like that. I'm getting you out of here."

"All right, Custis," Juan said, glancing over at the dim outline of Carlotta's crumpled body. "I will not talk like that."

Longarm took a deep, miserable breath. Never in his life would he be able to forget that scene he had witnessed from the ridge: Carlotta marching toward

17

the stream through a hail of lead, the bucket flying from her hand, then herself struck down, and Juan taking a slug himself as he dragged his wife back into the cabin. A turkey shoot was what that young whelp outside the cabin had called it. And, during all that horror, his only complaint was that he was too long away from his woman.

Longarm looked back at Juan. "The posse left someone out there by the corral to watch the cabin door. I shot him. Before the posse finds out he's not there, we've got a chance to get out of here. Maybe we can make it past the corral to the stream, then let it carry us down to the cottonwood flats. There are only two members of the posse down there, staying by the horses."

"We can take them easy," Juan said, the weakness in his voice clearly audible now.

Juan stirred himself and began to push himself erect. As he did so, he uttered a groan that seemed to have been wrung from his very soul. Reaching out quickly, Longarm helped him to his feet. Juan grabbed the windowsill with his good arm and managed a bleak grin.

"Don't touch the right arm, *amigo*," he warned Longarm. "When I pulled Carlotta inside, I made it worse than it was."

They moved toward the open doorway. When they reached it, Juan paused and looked down at his wife's crumpled body.

"We should not leave her like this," he said.

"I'll come back for her, Juan," Longarm said. "That's a promise."

Longarm's word was good enough for Juan. He

ducked before his friend out into the moonless night. Longarm followed. They kept low and reached the stream undetected. Longarm had to help Juan down the embankment and through the reeds. When Juan reached the icy waters and waded out into the stream, he kept going until the water reached his waist. Then he dipped his head and drank his fill.

Straightening then, Juan let the water take him downstream, holding onto his broken arm as he did so. Longarm kept by his side in case Juan should stumble and fall. Longarm had hung his gunbelt around his neck, and he held his Winchester out in front of him above the water. As long as he kept this close to the shore, his derringer was in no danger of getting wet.

They had not gone more than twenty yards when Longarm caught sight of the young man he had shot. The stream had carried his body into a shallow pool near the bank, but now the swift water was tugging at his legs. In a moment, it appeared, he would be swept back out into the stream.

Longarm slogged over and, grabbing the man by the back of his vest, dragged him up onto the embankment well out of the water. Then he leaned down to listen for a heartbeat, if there was one. There was, faint but steady. Inspecting the fellow's wounds, Longarm saw where the round had entered high on the left shoulder, shattering the collarbone. In the poor light he could not tell if the bullet had gone on through.

The young man's eyes flickered once, then opened. At the sight of Longarm bending over him, he started to raise himself and cry out. Longarm brought his fist around in a hard blow that caught the man flush on his chin. The jawbone cracked, and the fellow's eyes snapped shut again. Longarm stuffed the man's bandanna into the shoulder wound in an effort to stanch the flow of blood, then continued on down the stream after Juan.

He caught up with him just as they approached a sharp bend. Beyond this point the stream entered the flat, but the way was not clear. On a small bluff overlooking the stream, the two members of the posse who were guarding the horses had built a fire and were sitting before it, their rifles resting back against their shoulders.

Longarm tugged on Juan's shirt and indicated the embankment under the bluff. Juan nodded and waded toward it. The stream had cut well into the embankment before sluicing away into the flat, and its protective shadow soon fell over them as they clambered ashore. Both men were glad to get out of the icy water onto dry ground. Juan slumped down and closed his eyes almost at once. Longarm knelt on one knee beside him.

"I'm going up there to see to those two," Longarm told him softly. "Can you sit a horse?"

Juan nodded without opening his eyes.

There was still no moon, but Longarm was able to make out Juan's face clearly. It did not look good. The cold water had chilled him to the bone. His complexion was almost blue, and his teeth were chattering uncontrollably.

Longarm glanced up at the face of the embankment. He decided he would have to go around and come upon the two from the direction of the flat. Both men were sitting on the same side of the fire, facing the cabin upstream.

20

Leaving Juan, Longarm followed the stream's channel away from the bluff. Once he reached the flat, he slogged ashore once again, then dropped to the ground. The grass was tall and lush all the way to the crest of the bluff. Slipping his Winchester ahead of him along the ground, Longarm began to move through the tall grass with the stealth and patience of a large mountain cat after a long winter.

Chapter 3

Labeau and Slim were both unhappy at the prospect of spending another long night in this chill high country. But at least they had a fire.

Labeau, heavier and taller than Slim, was the darker and older of the two. Staring into the fire, he was considering what they were about. For the last six years, Slim and he had stuck closely to Clint Swenson. He was a man who knew how to find the slick opportunities—and even some that weren't so slick.

Along with a few other riders, last spring they had joined Clint in his ride north into this high country. They were on the lookout not only for soft touches, but also for distance from the Texas Rangers. Clint had found the ripe opportunity he was looking for with his election to the post of sheriff in Cody. With the power the job gave him, he was not only in a position to milk the county, but to take care of Labeau and Slim.

The trouble was, this crazy vendetta of Murchison's was in danger of getting out of hand. If Clint wasn't careful, this business could louse things up, even bring in a federal marshal. In something like this, the quickest way was always the best.

And Clint had missed out on that quick, decisive stroke a couple of days ago when he had botched an opportunity to bushwhack the greaser just outside Cody. To make matters worse, after trailing Romero all the way up here, Clint had let that greenhorn Pete Bushnell open fire too soon. It was that fool play that had let the Mexican make it the rest of the way to his cabin.

So now the son of a bitch was still holed up in there, and still trouble—a treed wildcat.

Labeau had a gut-deep feeling about this business. They had better get rid of Romero soon. They had caught the greaser for sure that last time, along with his woman, but it hadn't been pretty. Slim had admitted that it had been his shot that caught her. He had tried to scare her with a bullet past her cheek. Labeau shook his head at the thought. Sometimes he wondered about Slim.

Shifting restlessly on the log, Labeau reached over for a stick and poked at the fire. Winter came fast in this high country, and he could feel its chill on his neck already.

"You thinking what I'm thinking?" Slim asked.

Labeau turned to face him. "Sure, Slim," he said. "You're thinking it's getting pretty damn cold up here, and this operation is turning into work. Right?"

Slim grinned crookedly at his partner and nodded

emphatically. His long, shaggy blond hair hung down over one side of his face, giving him a mongrel look that added some to the menace he inspired in others.

"You put your finger on it, Labeau. Me for the warmer spots. I think I'd rather burn to death than freeze to death."

"If we go south," Labeau commented sardonically, "more'n likely we'll hang. So give it one more day, Slim. If this goes bad, maybe we'll have no choice but to quit this high country."

"You worried?"

"Sure I am. This is getting messy."

"What about Clint?"

"He's the sheriff now, all legal and proper. So I reckon he just might stay on here and keep milkin' Murchison and his Big Outfit."

"Clint won't milk Murchison if he don't get this greaser's scalp for him."

Labeau nodded. "And I'm sure Clint knows that."

"Which means," Slim went on gloomily, "that sooner or later, one of us is going to have to go into that cabin after the Mex."

"Not me," said Labeau, his swarthy face growing darker with resolve. "Not me. Lomax, maybe. Or that kid, Bushnell."

"Yeah. And I'm bettin' on Bushnell. All he wants is to impress his boss and get back to that woman of his. He's so eager to get out of here that Clint could march him into hell with a broom on his shoulder."

Labeau nodded glumly. Maybe what Slim said was true, but Labeau could not forget that it was Bushnell's early, too-hasty shot that had put them all in this pickle to begin with.

"Leastways," said Slim, shifting on the log and leaning closer to the fire, "we got the greaser's woman."

"You mean *you* did. But it's the greaser Murchison wants, not his woman."

A chill wind came off the peaks behind them. Labeau pulled his poncho closer about his lean shoulders and found himself thinking of the long trail up from Texas and the sleepy cowtowns along the way. Most of them were already full up with sodbusters and their nits, and the women with their bonnets and cold stares.

The country was getting too damn civilized. They had had to cut through more and more barbed wire after Abilene. Barbed wire. Labeau shook his head at the thought. And the telegraph. That really turned him grizzly. Like Clint told them, the damned telegraph and the federal marshals made it near impossible to get clean away from a raise.

Labeau shook his head at the thought. As he did so, he thought he heard something behind him. He started to turn.

The dark one turned just as Longarm clubbed the fellow with the long, shaggy blond hair sitting beside him. As the blond settled soundlessly off the log and crumpled forward into the fire, Longarm brought up the stock of his Winchester, catching the taller one on the side of the chin. The man was sent reeling back, one foot stomping down into the fire. Sparks showered upward, enclosing the man as he tried to twist away from Longarm.

Longarm stepped swiftly after him and brought his Colt around with punishing force, catching him on the side of the face and raking the barrel across the man's cheekbone. The fellow was unconscious before he struck the ground.

Holstering his Colt, Longarm pulled the lanky blond out of the fire. The fellow's shirt was smoldering and the flesh on his neck had begun to pucker. Longarm used the man's rifle to prop him back up on the log. Then he dragged his companion over and hunched him up on the log beside his friend. After throwing a few more logs on the fire, he moved back down the bluff to the stream.

He found Juan still lying face down on the bank. For a moment Longarm was afraid that Juan was unconscious. But as soon as Longarm reached his side, Juan opened his eyes and looked up at him, a slight smile flickering on his face.

"What took you so long, *amigo?* There were only two of them."

Longarm reached down and helped Juan to his feet. The man compressed his lips to keep from crying out when Longarm inadvertently touched his broken arm. Fashioning a sling for it with his bandanna, Longarm helped Juan to splash through the shallow stream bed and out onto the flat.

The horses were bunched in the shadow of a cottonwood grove close beside the stream. Longarm caught sight of the dim huddle of saddles in a heap under one of the trees. He let Juan down so he could rest with his back against a tree and then, working swiftly in the darkness, took the hobbles off each horse and saddled two of them. Helping Juan onto one of the two, he handed the reins up to Juan's good left hand.

"My horse is on the trail above the valley," he told

Juan. "Can you find the trail?"

"I can find it."

"I'll give you a start before I scatter the horses."

Juan nodded, clapped his heels feebly to the flanks of his mount, and started across the flat. Longarm watched until Juan disappeared into the night. Then he mounted up, rode over to the rest of the horses, and herded them away from the cottonwoods. Levering a fresh cartridge into his Winchester's firing chamber, he fired into the air. In a single plunging mass, the horses bolted away from him. Levering rapidly, he continued firing into the air as he galloped after them. Necks stretching, the horses surged into a full gallop. In a moment they were strung out ahead of him in the darkness.

He pulled up and listened.

From behind him came faint shouts. Ahead of him he heard the rapidly dying thunder of the stampeding animals. Longarm knew this valley well enough to know that there would be no barrier to their headlong flight for at least a couple of miles. If they found the Peace River pass, they would be in Sweetwater country by morning.

The shouting behind him was getting louder. Longarm turned his horse and galloped through the darkness after Juan.

The moment Pete Murchison saw Clint Swenson and his Texas sidekicks ride wearily through the Double M gate, the cattleman knew there was trouble. His daughter Cathy had seen them too. She hurried from the stable and joined her father as Swenson pulled up and dismounted wearily in front of them. His riders

28

stopped behind the sheriff and remained in their saddles, watching.

It was Cathy who spoke first, her voice laced with contempt. "I can tell from the set of your shoulders, Sheriff, that you botched it. The greaser got away."

Clint Swenson thumbed his hat back off his forehead, revealing his thick shock of yellow hair, and squared his shoulders. He was as tall as Murchison, heavily built, and still powerful. At the moment his blue eyes blazed back at the girl. But she was right. His news was bad, and that gave her the edge.

Swenson shrugged unhappily as he reported to Murchison. "The greaser had a friend, looks like. We don't know where in hell he came from, but he hit us while we was bottlin' up the Mex in his cabin. He shot up Pete Bushnell, busted his jaw, then stampeded our horses."

Murchison glanced past Swenson at Labeau and his sidekick, Slim. The two men looked bad—very bad. A mean gash had laid open Labeau's right cheekbone, and the side of his face had swollen to the color and consistency of an overripe plum.

Slim's eyes were red-rimmed and bleary. He seemed to have trouble focusing them. There were burn marks on his neck, and it was obvious that he had been struck a fearful blow on the skull. Murchison had once seen a similar look on the face of a blacksmith who had been kicked by a mule. The blacksmith had never regained his former efficiency.

Murchison looked incredulously at the sheriff. "Did that fellow have anything to do with the condition of these two?"

Swenson nodded gloomily. "Labeau and Slim were

guarding the horses. When we found them, both of them were unconscious. They weren't much help at all in rounding up the horses."

"You say one man did all this?"

Swenson shifted his feet nervously. "We only found one set of tracks."

"Well, just who was this fellow?"

"Damned if I know. That Mex didn't have no friends around here that I know of."

"What did he look like?" Cathy demanded. "Surely Slim or Labeau here could give us a description."

"It was dark, ma'am," Labeau mumbled.

Swallowing unhappily, Slim said, "I can't remember what happened."

"What about Pete?" Cathy demanded.

"He's got a shot-up collarbone and a busted jaw. He ain't been able to do nothing but groan. We had to leave him back there."

"And what about Juan Romero?"

Clint Swenson took a deep breath. "He got clean away, looks like. But we wounded him at least once. I saw him get hit myself."

Obviously anxious to bring some good news, Labeau said, "Anyway, we got the greaser's wife."

"You what?" demanded Cathy.

"We killed the Mex's wife," Swenson admitted ruefully.

Murchison took off his hat and ran his hand slowly over his face as he fought to keep his temper under control. Then he peered at Swenson. "Damnation," he whispered hoarsely. "Damnation! You let an unknown stranger tear up two of your men like this, wound Pete Bushnell, stampede your horses, free Juan Romero—the man who murdered my son—and then

moved, but Longarm could hear nothing. He leaned closer.

"Carlotta..." Juan whispered through cracked lips. "Don't leave her."

Longarm patted his friend's shoulder. When Juan tried to raise his arm to pull Longarm still closer, the deputy restrained him gently. "Take it easy now," he said. "No hurry about that. I can't leave you here like this."

The man's eyes became suddenly bright and for a brief moment they seemed to pierce Longarm's soul. "Yes...can leave me...soon."

Longarm was about to argue with him, but he did not have the heart for it. He placed his hand on Juan's forehead. Juan was burning up. The dying man spoke the truth. He was already halfway to hell, and he knew it.

Longarm felt a deep, bitter frustration. It had been a long ride he had made, only to find at the end of it that he must bury his friend. The desolate ache he had been living with this past night now became almost intolerable.

During the first year Longarm had journeyed West, he had found himself in some scrapes near the border. He had been in the middle of one particularly nasty encounter in a small border cantina when Juan dealt himself in. The man had saved him, and the two had become fast friends thereafter, emptying many a bottle together on the trail and in too many border towns where the only safety lay in a good friend and a well-oiled revolver. They had become closer than brothers.

Juan stirred and groaned suddenly, pulling Longarm back to the present.

Longarm reached for his canteen, unstoppered it,

and placed its tip in Juan's mouth. The man drank in short, convulsive gulps. When he began to cough, Longarm pulled the canteen away. Juan managed a smile.

"That was good, *amigo*. After all these years, you are still my friend, eh?" He reached out and caught Longarm's wrist, then pulled him closer with surprising strength. "You will see to those butchers. . . ."

"Yes, Juan," Longarm replied quietly. "I will. I will see to all of them."

Juan released Longarm's hand and sank back, nodding his head and closing his eyes. He seemed to breathe easier. "That is good, my friend," he murmured softly.

He grew quiet. Longarm again placed his open palm on Juan's forehead. The man was still burning up. A quick inspection of the chest wound told Longarm why. The wound had gone black around the edges. He had cleaned it as best he could, but it had done no good. It was festering. He could smell it. And there was nothing Longarm could do.

After a moment of contemplating Juan's wasted features, Longarm got wearily to his feet, went back to the line shack's doorway, and looked out at the cold, sunlit morning. A lark's bright call echoed in the meadow below the pines, its flight song an unsettling contrast to the grim business on the cot behind him. The clean sparkle of the mountain morning seemed only to increase Longarm's sense of loss.

Longarm heard Juan groan softly and call his name. He turned swiftly and hurried back into the shack.

At mid-morning of that same day, Longarm placed his hat back on and walked slowly away from the freshly turned earth that covered Juan Romero. Longarm had selected what he felt was a suitable spot—a grassy ledge overlooking a long, gentle sweep of parkland. It extended to the forested slopes of two snowcapped peaks that shouldered magnificently into the high, clean air. With such headstones, he felt, Juan and Carlotta would sleep well.

As he rode off a few minutes later to bring Carlotta back to join her husband, he thought again of that promise he had made to Juan to find and punish those butchers. When he remembered that promise, he felt a welcome, reckless rage. He could taste it, feel it take control of him.

It was almost enough rage to mask the deep, hammering grief he felt.

Longarm could see Carlotta's body just inside the doorway. It was late that same afternoon and, as Longarm glanced skyward, he saw a single buzzard coasting high overhead. Dismounting, he moved quickly into the cabin and past Carlotta's body to fetch a sheet and some blankets.

He was pulling them off the bed when the cabin doorway darkened behind him. Longarm spun around to see the young man from the posse he had dragged from the stream the night before. That had obviously been a fool weak thing to have done, and Longarm was sorry for it now—abysmally sorry.

The man had a gun in his hand and was leaning shakily against the doorjamb while he glared murderously at Longarm through pain-slitted eyes. He was as silent as death, standing there, and Longarm remembered the crack when he broke the man's jaw.

For a long moment the two stared at each other.

Then, shakily, but with grim purpose and an iron re-solve, the young man raised the gun and sighted along its barrel. Longarm did not wait a second longer. Throwing himself to one side, he drew his .44, clear-ing leather so swiftly that even as the gun thundered in the wounded man's hand, Longarm's own gun was coming up.

As the bullet slammed into the wall behind Long-arm, the man took a wooden step into the cabin and fired straight ahead a second time, then a third time. Longarm kept down to one side, watching, as the injured man continued to plod blindly forward, still pulling off shot after shot. Just as he reached the wall, the hammer came down on an empty chamber. The fellow stumbled forward against the wall, then slid down it to the floor.

Longarm holstered his weapon and stepped quickly to the unconscious man's side and turned him over. The fellow's eyes were wide open, but he did not see Longarm. He would see nothing living again.

A quick examination showed Longarm why. The bullet that had shattered his shoulder had not gone on through. It had angled down into his chest, most likely lodging in his lungs. Longarm rolled the young man back over onto his face, snatched the sheets and blan-ket off the bed, and hurried over to Carlotta's body.

Working swiftly, he bundled Carlotta up, draped her over the pommel, and swung into the saddle. That was when he heard the soft thunder of horses' hooves crossing the flat below the cabin. That dead man's gunshots were bringing whoever it was at a gallop. At once Longarm realized who they must be—the Double M's Texas gunslingers, coming back for their wounded man.

Longarm rowelled his mount into the timber above the cabin, flung himself from his horse, tied it up securely, then snaked his Winchester from its scabbard along with a couple of boxes of shells from his saddlebag. He moved swiftly back until he could see the cabin through the trees. Moving more cautiously after that, he found a big pine at the edge of the timber, broke open the boxes of shells, and levered a cartridge into the Winchester's firing chamber.

Then he waited.

He did not have long to wait. Four riders and a woman driving a flatbed wagon pounded up to the cabin. The riders dismounted and one of them, obviously the leader, strode into the cabin to return almost at once with the news of what he had found. At that moment one of the other riders, who was down on one knee studying the ground, called out sharply. At once the four riders remounted and started to follow Longarm's tracks toward the timber. Longarm could not be sure, but he was almost certain he could hear the woman's shrill voice urging them on.

He fitted the rifle stock to his shoulder, sighted carefully along the barrel, and fired. The foremost rider spun off his horse and disappeared into the thick, tufted grass. Longarm levered swiftly and fired a second time, putting the remaining riders into frantic flight back toward the cabin.

The woman, still on her seat in the flatbed, appeared furious at their good sense and began screaming at them to go back. Longarm aimed carefully at a spot just in front of her team of horses and fired. Even at that distance he could see the spurt of dust that kicked up at the horses' feet. With a shrill whinny, the startled horses reared in their traces. Longarm fired again. This time the woman leaped from the wagon and joined the others in a flight to the cabin.

Longarm put two quick shots through the open doorway and then bellied down beside the tree. There was no sign of movement from the man he had dropped with his first shot. He dismissed him, put his sights on the already shattered window over the kitchen, pulled off just a little bit, then fired. He heard the smack of the slug in the logs, waited a moment for the warning to sink in, then put two quick shots through the window. He moved his sights and put another shot through the doorway, levering a fresh cartridge into the firing chamber, and waited.

He could hear the murmur of unhappy voices coming from the cabin. Abruptly, there was a shot, followed by the thunk of a bullet as it lodged in the tree just above his head. Longarm moved farther back behind the tree and then put two more shots through the window. Loud, bitter cursing followed this exchange. Then came silence.

Longarm reached into his pocket and pulled out a cheroot. Lighting it, he sucked the smoke into his lungs and glanced swiftly about him. It was getting chilly and would soon be dark. Already a cold upland mist was moving along the surface of the stream and across the flats below the cabin.

A head appeared in the cabin window. Longarm sighted swiftly and squeezed off a shot. A chip of wood from the windowsill flew into the air. Before Longarm could fire again, whoever it was had ducked back out of sight. When no one else poked a head up to look out, Longarm realized they had received his message.

He was still out here, and still watching.

Dusk came on swiftly after that. As it deepened, Longarm put occasional shots into the cabin, just to impress upon its huddled occupants his accuracy and his persistence—and to give them just a small taste of what the siege must have been like for Juan and Carlotta.

At last, as darkness settled finally over the valley, Longarm sent four quick shots at the cabin, waited a moment or two, then rose and faded back into the timber. Reaching his mount, he untied it and vaulted into the saddle, guiding the animal through the timber as swiftly as the fading light would allow.

He did not expect any difficulty in finding his way back to the line shack, nor was he worried about those men behind him being able to follow his trail in the dark. They would not be able to track him until morning. And when they reached the place where he had buried Juan and Carlotta sometime tomorrow, Longarm would be well on his way into Cody.

He needed to know more than the dying Juan had been able to tell him. That meant he would have to seek out the lawyer who had defended Juan, and perhaps the judge who had dismissed the murder charge for lack of evidence. The lawyer's name was Landon. Longarm had not been able to catch the name of the judge. According to Juan, both men had shown great courage in standing up to the Big Outfit and freeing Juan despite Murchison's threats.

Perhaps Landon could tell Longarm enough for him to telegraph to Billy Vail for warrants. Last night, before the fever had rendered him incoherent, Juan had described the new sheriff of Cody and his deputies as Texans. There was some talk in town that they had been imported by Murchison to keep sodbusters off his grass. Perhaps this Clint Swenson and his deputies had left Texas for a good reason.

But, warrants or no warrants, whatever it took, Longarm would see to those men behind him in the darkness—see to them as finally and as ruthlessly as they had seen to Juan and Carlotta Romero.

Chapter 4

Longarm was standing on the porch of the Big Country Saloon when Cathy Murchison turned the flatbed wagon onto Front Street. The two blanketed corpses in the wagon bed had already been spotted, and the news had swept ahead of her. By this time, everyone on Front Street knew what she was bringing to town.

Longarm moved to the edge of the porch and leaned against a porch pillar, drawing reflectively on his cheroot as he watched the girl.

He was mightily impressed by her beauty. The bright white silk of her blouse was in startling contrast to her wide-brimmed black hat and split skirt. She had long chestnut hair and strong, rather than pretty, features. At the moment, she presented a grim, formidable appearance. Keeping her dark eyes straight ahead, she did her best to ignore those keeping up with her wagon along the board sidewalks and the barefoot urchins racing down the street ahead of her.

A few horsemen riding in the opposite direction turned their horses as she passed so they could gain a better view of the two corpses in the back of the wagon. Longarm could see that the blanket had worked itself off the head of the young man he had been forced to kill, and he wondered if the other one might be the fellow he had knocked off his mount the afternoon before.

An excited ranch hand clambered up onto the porch, brushed past Longarm, and poked his head in through the batwings.

"Looks like Cathy Murchison's bringing in that greaser's body!" he cried.

At once the saloon emptied. As the patrons flowed around Longarm, angling for a view into the bed of the wagon, the girl pulled up in front of the barbershop across from the saloon. As she did so, Longarm stepped off the porch and crossed the street to get a clearer view of Cathy Murchison. He was more than a little curious about her, remembering vividly her shrill, furious cries as she urged those four riders into the timber after him.

Cathy climbed down from the wagon and paused wearily. The barber was standing on the porch, a foam-flecked straight razor in his hand.

"Burnside," the girl called up to him, "where's Doc Fletcher?"

"I'm comin', Cathy," said a voice from above them.

Longarm turned to see the doctor coming down the outside stairs from his office over the barbershop. He

42

was a tall, spare man with gaunt, prominent cheekbones and eyes that seemed to be looking out at the world from the depths of an ancient despair. He looked drunk to Longarm, and he probably was, but he appeared to be capable of holding his liquor well.

As the doctor stepped off the boardwalk to approach Cathy Murchison, another man joined him. This man Longarm already knew to be Tim Landon, the lawyer who had defended Juan. Cathy ignored Landon pointedly as she addressed the doctor.

"I've got two dead men in this wagon, Doc," she said coldly. "Pete Bushnell and Billy Lester."

An excited murmur ran through the crowd. A few hurried off to spread the news. The doctor nodded as casually as if the girl had just told him she had a slight cold. He glanced into the wagon, then looked back at her.

"I'll see to the death certificates," he told her. "Burnside will see to the burial." Brushing his yellowing mustache with a long forefinger, he raised his eyebrows in silent interrogation.

"No, the greaser is not dead. The man who killed my brother is still alive. And I am certain it was a gunslick the greaser hired who killed Pete and Billy."

Her words caused a further sensation, and more members of the crowd peeled off to spread the news.

"The Double M will see to the funeral expenses, Doc," Cathy went on, ignoring the commotion, "if you and Burnside would please take these bodies for me. I have to go find Carol Bushnell."

At that moment Marshal Brad Borrman hustled through the crowd, his ample gut cutting a wide swath as he plowed ahead. The lawyer Landon was about to say something to Cathy Murchison, but Borrman brushed him coldly aside as he pulled up in front of the girl.

"How'd it happen, Miss Murchison?" the town marshal boomed.

"Not here, Mr. Borrman," she replied curtly. "And not until I speak to Carol Bushnell. I'll see you in your office later."

"Why, sure thing, Miss Murchison."

The lawyer stepped close than and again started to say something to the girl, but before he could get a word out, she snapped, "I don't want to hear a word from you, Tim Landon! It's your fault, all of this. Pete Bushnell and Billy Lester would be alive now if you hadn't prevented us from hanging that killer. Their blood is on your hands!"

Her voice carried far and the crowd was hushed as every man and woman in it strained to catch each word. Longarm saw Tim Landon step back as if he had been struck. He had obviously not been prepared for Cathy Murchison's outburst. But he spoke not a word of reproach. Murmuring politely, he touched his hatbrim to her, then stepped aside to let her pass.

But his courtesy only seemed to arouse her to a greater pitch. "You are through in this county, Mr. Landon," she told him, her voice laced with scorn. "You'll get no further business from the Double M or any of the other ranchers. And Judge Kyle is only one more elected official. You can tell him that for me. The Double M will handle the justice in this county from now on—the way men are supposed to handle it!"

"I'll tell him that, Miss Murchison," Landon replied with icy dignity.

"See that you do!"

"That's tellin' him!" someone in the crowd behind Longarm shouted approvingly.

Immediately, other bystanders joined in that sentiment. It was clear to Longarm that the citizens of Cody, like Cathy Murchison, were absolutely convinced that Juan Romero had murdered Cathy's brother—and that Tim Landon had only served to obstruct justice when he defended him successfully in court. Like everyone else, it seemed, Cathy Murchison was entirely wrong about Juan Romero—tragically wrong—but she was far too headstrong to listen to reason.

Longarm watched the girl stride angrily past Tim Landon and hurry down the wooden sidewalk. A moment later, she ran into the arms of a girl waiting for her in front of a small dress shop. Sobbing, the two women hurried into the dress shop together.

Longarm felt a twinge. The woman waiting in front of the dress shop was undoubtedly Pete Bushnell's widow.

Sitting at a table in the rear of the saloon a moment later, Longarm watched Tim Landon enter. A momentary hush fell over the place as the young lawyer strode to the bar and ordered a whiskey. Turning with his drink, he leaned back against the bar and sipped it. He was careful, Longarm noted, not to meet any eyes directly. He knew how unwelcome he was in this place, but he was too much of a man to let it keep him out. Longarm was as impressed by this as he was by the calm and dignified way the lawyer had taken Cathy Murchison's tongue-lashing.

Just as Longarm was about to stir himself and approach Landon to introduce himself, the town marshal burst into the saloon with a big fellow wearing a sheriff's star and two of his sidekicks. Marching up to the bar, the marshal slammed a meaty hand down upon it to gain everyone's attention.

"Drinks are on me, boys!" Borrman cried. "The greaser is dead—and so is his woman. Clint here found their graves!"

With a rush, the saloon's patrons left their chairs and swarmed up to the bar. Longarm stayed where he was, bitterness filling him. It did him no good to see these jackals celebrating the death of Juan and his wife. Tim Landon was another who did not join Swenson at the bar. Taking his drink with him, Landon found an empty table along the wall, sat down, and watched the back-slapping gang at the bar with a bitter, sardonic smile on his face.

Borrman, a foaming stein of beer held high in his right hand, turned about and caught sight of Landon.

"Well, now!" the man cried. "Lookee who's here! Ain't you goin' to drink with the sheriff, counselor?" Borrman asked insolently. "Ain't you goin' to celebrate? This time justice was done, with none of your fancy talk to prevent it."

Landon shook his head angrily. "No, damn you, Borrman," he said, his voice trembling with indignation. "I'll be damned if I'll drink with Swenson and his hired killers!"

Borrman started toward the lawyer, his eyes angry slits. "You'll drink with us—or else!"

Landon jumped to his feet and flung away his shot-glass, doubling his fists as he did so. But Borrman's huge ham of a hand snaked out and grabbed Landon by his shirtfront and flung him brutally to one side.

Landon's foot caught on the leg of a chair, and both he and the chair went over.

Glaring down at Landon, the marshal said, "You ain't in no courtroom now, Landon. And they ain't no judge nearby to shut me up, neither. So when you call the sheriff and his men killers, I call that disturbin' the peace."

Furious, exhibiting more courage than discretion, Landon scrambled to his feet and rushed Borrman. But the big town marshal brought his fist around with swift precision, catching Landon on his right cheek. Landon spun wildly and hit the floor face down. Raising himself groggily, he shook his head to clear it. Borrman stepped back and waited patiently. As soon as Landon pushed himself erect again, he stepped in close and began punishing the young lawyer with solid, measured blows that drove Landon relentlessly toward the wall.

Watching, Longarm winced. There seemed nothing Landon could do to protect himself. When Landon brought up his fists to cover his face, Borrman would drive sledging blows to Landon's midsection. At last, with brutal efficiency, the town marshal finished Landon off. Stepping inside the lawyer's futile, ineffective punches, he countered with two solid, sledging blows that caught Landon flush on the side of his jaw. Landon went down like a stone.

Sheriff Swenson's blond sidekick hurried over then and pulled Borrman away. His eyes were alight with anticipation. "You've had your fun, Brad," he told the town marshal. "Now it's my turn. He called us killers, don't forget. Wouldn't want to make a liar out of him."

As he spoke, he pulled back his booted foot and lashed out viciously, catching Landon on the side of the head. Landon's eyes popped open, then shut, like a doll that just been dropped on the floor. Fully aroused now, the slim, blond fellow kicked Landon repeatedly about the head and shoulders.

Then his comrade, the dark, curly-haired one whose face Longarm had ripped with the barrel of his .44, stepped up to take his licks. Pushing the friend aside, he hauled the barely conscious lawyer upright.

Longarm had seen enough—more than enough. Jumping to his feet, he called sharply across the saloon, "Leave him alone! If you want someone to play with, try me!"

The Texan paused, blinking in disbelief at Longarm. "You crazy, mister? Takin' this fool's part?"

"I said leave him be! If you lay a hand on that man, it just might be murder. Can't you see he's already been hurt bad?"

"Oh, is that so? Isn't that terrible!"

The curly-haired one let go of the lawyer. Landon fell to the floor, his head striking with a crack loud enough to bring a sudden hush to the place. The sheriff stepped quickly away from the bar and placed himself between Longarm and his two sidekicks.

This was the first time Longarm had been able to get a good look at the man who had led that posse outside Juan's cabin. The Texan favored a buckskin jacket and was a lean, cold-eyed fellow with yellow hair combed straight back. It almost reached to his shoulders.

Smiling thinly at Longarm, Swenson said, "Guess you got a point there, stranger. The counselor's had enough punishment this time, looks like."

With a shrug, the two men left the downed lawyer and returned to the bar. Clint Swenson looked carefully at Longarm. "Is Tim Landon a friend of yours, stranger?"

"Never saw him before today."

"Just rode in, did you?"

"That's right."

"Well, this poor son of a bitch is your bunk mate now, mister. Get him out of here. This here's a cattleman's bar. It ain't no proper place for him—or for you, neither. And hurry it up. The counselor's beginning to stink up the place."

Grimly, Longarm picked his way through the wreckage of tables and chairs, bent down, and slung the now unconscious Landon over his shoulder. The young man was surprisingly frail—almost as light as a bird. Turning gently with his burden, Longarm left the saloon, crossed the street to the barbershop, and mounted the outside steps to the doctor's office.

Knocking once, Longarm opened the door and entered. Inside, he found a small waiting room with the doctor's office the next room in. Beyond it, he glimpsed a long, narrow room that contained at least four army cots.

Doc Fletcher poked his head out of his office and took in Longarm's burden at a glance. "In here," he told Longarm, getting up from his desk and moving ahead of him into the room containing the cots.

The doctor paused by the first cot, his long, cadaverous face assuming a weary cast. Longarm put Landon down as gently as he could and stepped back. The doctor bent over his patient for a quick examination. Shaking his head in dismay, he straightened.

"Who did this?" he asked.

"Borrman. And he had help from one of the sheriff's sidekicks—a lanky blond fellow."

"That'd be Slim Ratch."

"He had a friend who wanted to join in also."

"Dark curly hair and a mean light in his eye?"

Longarm nodded.

"That'd be Curly Labeau. Two hardcases. Tim Landon was kicked. Who did that?"

"Slim Ratch."

"Of course."

Bending once again to inspect Landon, the doctor probed the lawyer's skull expertly and gently. He did not seem to like what his fingers told him. Landon groaned and stirred fitfully. As he started to raise himself up, the doctor restrained him gently. Landon opened his eyes and tried to focus on the doctor.

"You've got a pretty nasty crack on your head, Landon," the doctor told him, "and maybe a broken rib or two. Just lie still, there. And that's an order."

Squinting, Landon looked past the doctor at Longarm, then frowned quickly, as if the simple act of focusing his eyes had cost him dearly. Groaning he looked back at the doctor.

"You're right, doc. I got an awful headache."

"You should see your face," replied the doctor. "If you feel as bad as you look, you'd better lie still."

Landon nodded slightly and closed his eyes. The doctor pulled an army blanket up around him, and beckoning to Longarm, went out of the room. Closing the door softly, he told the lawman, "After he's got some rest and his headache lets up some, I'll bind those ribs of his." He shook his head and frowned. "He should be all right in a couple of weeks, depending

50

on just how serious that head injury is." He looked sharply at Longarm. "There is a mean welt just above Landon's temple, but the temple itself is not damaged. Did something hit him on the back of the head?"

"I didn't like what I saw, so I told Labeau to back off. Labeau had hold of Landon at the time and he just let him go. The back of Landon's head came down hard on the floor."

"That might be it, then." He shook his head. "Them two—Labeau and Slim—they make quite a team."

Fletcher opened his bottom desk drawer and lifted out a bottle of whiskey and two glasses. He poured himself two fingers, then glanced at Longarm.

"The same," Longarm replied.

The doctor poured and handed Longarm his drink. "Looks like we'll just have to wait and see. Landon might get through this with only a headache. And then again . . ." The doctor shrugged wearily, tossed down his drink, then looked at Longarm again.

"You're new in town, mister, that right?"

Longarm nodded.

"You got a name?"

"Long. Custis Long."

"I think I better tell you, Long, that when you mixed in this business between Landon and the sheriff, you bought yourself a peck of trouble."

"Maybe."

"No question about it."

"Thanks, doc. I'll be back later to check on Landon. Does he have any kin in town or hereabouts I should notify?"

"Not a one."

"Thanks for the drink," Longarm said. Sticking a

cheroot in his mouth, he pulled open the door and left the doctor's office.

About an hour later Longarm was sitting in the anteroom outside Judge Kyle's office, waiting for the man to drive his buggy in from his small ranch outside of Cody. The judge's secretary was a pretty girl in a flowered dress with a large bow at her neck and a pile of heavy chestnut hair on top of her head. She did what she could to appear busy, but she could not seem to keep her eyes off Longarm, and Longarm found himself with the same problem.

But it was a minor problem. For the moment, Longarm was pretty well preoccupied. After leaving the doctor's office, he had gone straight to the land office to get a copy of the deed Juan and he had obtained for their land. He was anxious to check it over and make certain it was recorded properly. It was—and that made Deputy U.S. Marshal Custis Long, as the only surviving partner, the owner of the J Bar Ranch.

Searching further in the records, he found that the three small ranches that once stood between Juan's ranch and Murchison's Double M were no longer on the map. They had either been bought out or abandoned. With the J Bar out of his way, Murchison would have nothing between his range and the Sweetwater.

The land agent had not made it difficult for Longarm to pry from him the reason for the disappearance of the other spreads. In each case, it seemed, the offending ranchers had been accused of rustling Big M stock, and the evidence against each had been so convincing that, rather than fight the Big Outfit, they had either sold out to Murchison or simply fled the valley.

Juan had refused to sell out, and he had kept his fences so well patroled that Murchison was unable to pin anything on him.

Until the death of Murchison's son Jed, that is.

What Longarm tried to figure out now, as he sat waiting for the judge, was the connection between Jed Murchison's death and this attempt on the Big Outfit to gain Juan's ranch and access to the Sweetwater. Certainly Murchison would not have had his own son killed simply to generate an excuse for getting Juan off the J Bar.

The judge pushed open the door and walked in. He glanced at Longarm, then smiled at his secretary.

"This is Mr. Custis Long," she said. "He would like to see you. I told him it would be all right to wait."

"Quite right, Mary. Quite right."

The judge turned to Longarm. He was a tall, formidable gentleman in a derby hat and a long frock coat. He had bushy gray eyebrows, a long, somber face, and eyes bright with intelligence and humor. Remembering what Juan had told him about the judge, Longarm liked the man at once.

Longarm got to his feet and the two men shook hands. The judge's grip was strong and unyielding.

"Mr. Long, is it?" the judge said. "Come into my chambers, sir, and tell me what it is you wish from the court."

Longarm followed the man inside, waited for him to close the door and hang his derby on a hat tree in the corner, then sat down in the chair beside the desk.

53

The judge walked around his desk and sat down.

"I've already heard about you, Mr. Long," he said somberly.

Longarm frowned.

"Juan Romero told me about you. He said you would come up here to vouch for his character. You did not fail him, I see. He also mentioned that you were now a deputy U.S. marshal operating out of Denver. I took the liberty of checking on you myself. I hope you don't mind. What I heard was good—very good. You do your job, it seems, and you do it well."

"Thank you."

The man's old face looked a bit older then. "I have just heard about Juan and Carlotta. The news got to me even before I reached town." He shook his head in disgust. "I expect dancing in the streets any moment now. It's enough to make a man sorry that he is a member of the human race. You have my sympathy, Long. I know how you must feel."

Longarm nodded.

"Now what can I do for you?" the judge went on.

"Judge, I just saw the town marshal and the sheriff of this county participate in the brutal beating of Tim Landon. It seems to me that we have here in Cody a breakdown of law and order. A U.S. marshal should be called in."

The old man gave Longarm a flinty grin and reached under his blotter. "Read this," he said, handing a copy of a telegram to Longarm. "I sent that yesterday."

Longarm read it. When he was finished, his eyebrows had gone up a notch. The judge had informed the territorial governor that, in his opinion, Sheriff Clint Swenson was no longer capable of keeping the peace, and he was requesting that a U.S. marshal be sent in to restore order.

Longarm handed the copy of the telegram back to the judge.

Taking it, the man said, "In addition, Mr. Long, I have convened the town council. We meet tonight. I intend to see to it that Brad Borrman is stripped of his badge. I know this will mean a confrontation with the Big Outfit, but this town and this county have danced to Pete Murchison's tune long enough."

"I'm glad to hear that," Longarm said.

The judge leaned back in his chair. "If the governor gives me the power to appoint you, would you be willing to clean up this county?"

This was precisely what Longarm had in mind. He nodded. "I'll get in touch with my chief, Billy Vail, in Denver," he said. "I don't think he'll mind. And he just might be able to track down a few warrants. Seems to me there must be a wanted poster out there somewhere with the descriptions of Clint Swenson, Curly Labeau, and Slim Ratch on it. They hail from Texas, I understand."

"Yes. That's right. Texas." The judge smiled. "That happens to be where I come from, also, Long."

"No aspersions meant."

"None taken."

Longarm got to his feet. "One other thing. As the new owner of the J Bar, I am going to do what I can to stir things up. I suggest that for now you keep my identity as a deputy U.S. marshal to yourself."

"Done. And let me give you a word of advice. Be careful. Murchison plays rough. He is not only greedy for land, but he is half out of his mind with the death of his son."

"Cathy Murchison, too, I noticed."

"Yes."

Longarm was at the door, pulling it open, when the judge called him back. He turned. The man was on his feet, watching him closely.

"I heard about the deaths of Pete Bushnell and Billy Lester, also. You wouldn't happen to know anything about that, would you?"

"I know all about it. I am also the one who buried Juan and Carlotta."

"I understand," he said grimly.

Longarm left the judge's chambers and closed the door. His secretary was very busy with some papers as he passed and did not look up. Longarm stopped in front of her desk and waited.

She glanced up at him, her face flushed.

He smiled down at her. "I'm a stranger in town. There are things I need to know. It seems to me a girl like you would be in the perfect position to know what's going on."

"You mean where the bodies are buried?"

"I didn't mean to put it that crudely," he said with a smile.

"Well, yes, I guess I do know what's going on," she said, flustered.

"I'd like to have dinner with you tonight. Would that be possible?"

Her face went scarlet. "It might."

"Do you live in town?"

"I live in a small cabin outside of town." Her face was still flushed, but there was an unmistakable glow of excitement in her eyes. "I put great store by my privacy, Mr. Long, and I hate gossips. I will expect you for supper at six. Follow the road out of town going north. Take the first cutoff. My cabin is on a gentle rise alongside the creek. There will be wood-smoke pouring out of the chimney by that time."

Longarm smiled, touched the brim of his hat to her, and left.

Chapter 5

Pete Murchison was furious. Cathy had never seen her father this angry.

Brad Borrman was standing sheepishly in front of her father's desk. Clint Swenson had made himself comfortable, as usual, in the big leather armchair to one side. Curly Labeau and Slim Ratch were leaning against the wall behind Clint. Cathy was sitting on the sofa, watching Borrman and her father.

It had been bad enough when she had ridden in with Carol Bushnell and told her father what Borrman and Clint's sidekicks had done to Tim Landon. But what Borrman had just said seemed to have been the last straw for the owner of the Double M.

"Let me get this straight," her father said, his voice deceptively calm. "You heard about the town council meeting coming up. So when you saw the judge on the street, you told him what he could do with his tin badge. Am I right? Is that what you just told me?"

No longer as cocksure as he had been a moment before, Borrman shifted uncomfortably and nodded. "That's right. When he said he had enough votes in the council meeting tonight, I just threw the badge at him. I don't need that piece of tin."

"You fool! You're not the one who needs it! I'm the one! As long as I owned you and you had that badge, whatever I did in that town was legal!"

Borrman shifted unhappily. "Mr. Murchison, you didn't own me."

"Like hell I didn't! It was my votes got you that job. I called in a lot of IOU's to put you in there and keep you on, no matter how much you drank or who you beat to a pulp on Saturday nights. And I might have been able to turn this around when I show up tonight if you hadn't quit!"

Borrman started to frame a reply, but lost heart before he got a word out. He looked miserably over at Clint for support, but the sheriff, Cathy noted, had become intensely interested in his hatband.

"Get out of here!" her father roared at Borrman, his patience at an end. "You too, Labeau—Slim. Go see Cookie if you're hungry. The three of you are welcome to sleep in the bunkhouse tonight. But I want all of you out of here first thing in the morning."

Borrman clapped his hat back on and shuffled unhappily out of the big room, Labeau and Slim following. When they were gone, Cathy's father looked bleakly over at Clint.

"I don't like it, Clint," he told the sheriff. "I've

60

just heard that Kyle has sent a telegram to the new territorial governor. He wants authority to replace you. I don't know this new governor. And it sounds to me like Kyle does."

"Or thinks he does."

"No matter. Damn it, Clint, did you have to stand idly by and let Borrman and Slim pick Landon apart like that? Beating up on that fool lawyer is no way for a town marshal to behave. And you were on hand throughout the thrashing. What the hell were you thinking of?"

"It's my fault," said Cathy, speaking up abruptly. "I'm to blame. The way I spoke to Tim in public gave every man in Cody a license to go after him. It is no surprise to me that Borrman and those two wasted no time in doing what they did. I take full responsibility."

Then she looked coldly at Clint.

"Tim was wrong in letting that murdering greaser go free. But, damn it, Clint, he's not a big man physically. He has more courage than brains. And Borrman is an animal. How could you have just stood there? Is that how it's done in Texas?"

"Cathy," her father said wearily, "ease up, will you? During all our trouble, it has been Clint who has stuck by our side. He came a long way to help us. It was a mistake for him to let Landon get beaten up like that, but you must admit, Tim certainly asked for trouble. What in blazes was he doing in that saloon in the first place? He knows the Big Country only caters to cattlemen."

"And he called us killers when we told the crowd we'd found Romero's grave," Clint added. He seemed anxious that Cathy should understand his position.

"I don't care, Clint," Cathy snapped. "It simply wasn't necessary to beat him like that."

"Cathy," her father said wearily. "Tim will be all right. He'll have a headache for a while and that'll be that. The important thing is that Juan Romero will no longer be picking our ranges clean—and that the murderer of my son and your brother has been duly avenged. At least we've gained that much."

There was no sense in arguing any further, she realized. She got up and left the room.

A moment later, without having to guide her footsteps, she found herself in what had been Jed's bedroom and office combined. She slumped, utterly drained, into his big wing chair by the window and tried to sort out her feelings.

She had thought that all she wanted was the death of that Mexican. And yet, when she heard what had happened to Tim in that saloon and hurried to the doc's office and saw how badly Tim had been punished, the rage that had fired her these past terrible weeks had drained from her completely, leaving her only confused and filled with a dismal emptiness.

It seemed that no matter what they did, no matter how many ranchers or nesters they fought off, others would always appear on their flanks to harry them still. She leaned back in her chair and looked out through the window at the lush coverlet of grassland that swept all the way to the peaks of the Wind River Range, the mighty capped battlement that protected their valley. It was a scene Jed had loved. It was why he had chosen this room for himself.

But now Jed was gone. And above her in this big lonely house, Carol Bushnell was in Cathy's room, weeping for the loss of her husband, while Cathy sat down here in this big chair watching the lengthening shadows fall across the range, bracing herself for whatever new trouble lay ahead for the Double M.

Longarm patted his stomach and pushed himself away from the table. He wanted to belch, but he didn't dare. "You are some cook, Mary," he told her, shaking his head. "I think I'll go find myself a nice warm hole and crawl in. I could sleep a year on that meal."

"It was the dumplings. You like apple dumplings, Custis Long."

"There wasn't anything wrong with that roast beef, either."

"You go in there and lie down on that couch and let me finish up here. Take a short nap, why don't you? I won't mind."

Stretching luxuriously, Longarm headed for the couch. "I just might do that," he told her. "Wake me up when you want me."

"Oh, I will," she said. "I will."

Longarm hit the couch and was asleep almost at once. It was not only the heaviness engendered by the meal—it was the cumulative exhaustion built up by the past week's events.

When he awoke, he found himself being led groggily into Mary's bedroom. She pushed him gently back onto the bed and proceeded to undress him. In a moment she was bent over his nakedness, her corset off, wearing only her shift. As he gaped, she stepped out of the shift and smiled at him.

"You had a nice nap," she told him. "Now it's time for you to thank me proper for that meal—and for all the information I am going to give you."

She fell forward onto his broad chest and nipped his earlobe.

"You still hungry?" he asked, his weariness falling away instantly as he closed his arms about her.

"For you I am."

"You do me honor," he replied as she swung her moist lips to his. For a long moment they just clung to each other, trying to melt into one another in the dark room.

He ran his free hand down her back, then under to the warm moisture between her trembling thighs. She groaned softly as Longarm parted her knees with his own. Rolling gently onto her, he moved up slightly and was in her. She gasped and moved her face to one side, sobbing, "It's been *so long!* So terribly long! Oh, God, how I needed you!"

"Hush," he murmured, his big hands on her buttocks, pulling her into him still deeper.

Clinging to him fiercely, she locked her thighs about his waist and lunged upward, shuddering. Longarm came fast, stayed inside her, and began moving gently, rhythmically, as their heaving flesh got better acquainted. She began to moan and rake her nails down his back, shuddering convulsively under him. Then her arms tightened about his neck. At last, uttering a high, keening wail, she came too.

Longarm was startled, but he kept on thrusting nevertheless. Her cry died as she clung weakly to him. She was game and, laughing softly up at him, began to thrust again. She dug her nails in still deeper and raised her knees until her heels were crossed behind his neck. He was hitting bottom with each stroke and he eased off a bit, aware that he could be hurting her. At once she hissed at him angrily and pumped hard to meet his thrusts.

"All of it! I want all of it inside me! Oh, Jesus, I want it again!"

He didn't know which of them she meant, but he was glad she wasn't going to scream this time. Then he just abandoned himself to the pleasure of it as they had a long, shuddering, mutual orgasm. She went limp. Longarm knew he was heavy so, after lying there long enough to catch his breath, he shifted his weight to his elbows and eased off some.

She sighed. "Don't move. Just let it soak inside me till we can do some more. You're still nice and hard. My, there certainly is a lot of you, isn't there?"

"It's been a while for me, too, Mary."

"You must think me an absolute wanton, but I don't care. I don't care if you think this is what I had in mind the moment you entered Judge Kyle's office."

He smiled and brushed back a lock of her auburn hair. "It's what I had in mind when I saw you behind that desk. I figure it was mutual—our attraction, that is."

"Oh, yes," she sighed happily. "That it was. I was so flustered! Did I blush?"

"You blushed."

"So you knew."

"I knew."

"Then let's do it again. But this time I want to be on top."

Longarm rolled off her and lay on his back. Smiling lasciviously, she climbed above him, placing a knee by each of Longarm's hip bones. She toyed with his moist erection for a moment, then guided herself onto it with both her hands. He leaned back and sighed with pleasure as she suddenly dropped her pelvis hard, taking it deep with a breathy hiss of her own.

And then she was thrusting up and down, riding him with a wild, incredible vitality. Grinning down at him suddenly, she leaned forward, swinging her nipples across Longarm's face.

"Suck me!" she cried. "Suck me!"

He caught one of her nipples between his lips. She went wild. He began rearing to meet her downward thrusts, and when he came it was like an eruption of molten lava. Uncoiling, he thrust high into the air. With that same keening cry she had let loose before, she flung herself forward onto him, hugging her breasts to his face, almost smothering him.

Then they rolled to one side, still locked in each other's arms.

When they came together again it was in her small living room, both of them fully dressed and presentable, with warm, contented smiles on their faces. Longarm sat in the big easy chair by the fireplace, puffing on a cheroot. Mary was curled up on the sofa.

Longarm asked her what she knew of the other ranchers who had obviously been driven out by the Double M.

"One of them was the Lazy S," she replied, with just a trace of bitterness in her voice. "It was my ranch—and my husband Jim's. When Murchison's men drove him from the valley, I decided to stay. I was sick of running. I am afraid that Jim, wherever he is, is still running."

66

"Did he rustle any of Murchison's cattle?"

"Yes," she said flatly. "I knew nothing about it, but Jim was a poor rancher, Longarm, and he had to make ends meet somehow. Murchison's men caught him working his running iron on their stock, and that made it rather easy for them."

"What about the other ranchers?"

"I'm not sure. But one thing *is* sure, Longarm. The Double M is losing cattle, and Murchison is beside himself trying to find out who's doing it."

"I see."

"But I know—and so did Judge Kyle and Tim Landon—that the J Bar was *not* rustling any of Murchison's stock. Juan didn't need to. He was doing fine on his own, minding his business and tending to his fences."

"There's no doubt, is there, that Murchison would like free range all the way to the Sweetwater?"

"None," she replied.

"Would that account for him framing Juan?"

"Possibly. But, I repeat, Murchison is losing cattle, and he is absolutely sincere in thinking Juan was responsible for his son's death."

"That doesn't make it right—what he and his men did."

"Of course not."

"What can you tell me about Murchison's daughter?" Longarm asked.

She smiled. "Beautiful, isn't she?"

"So is a cobra."

"Don't judge her too harshly. She and her brother Jed were very close. Between the two of them, they would have been able to run the Big Outfit quite successfully after their father passed on. Another thing: she was sort of engaged to Tim Landon before Jed's death. I am afraid there is no longer any chance of that now. Too bad."

"Tim's been hurt pretty bad, you know."

"I know."

Longarm got up. "It's late. I'd better be going."

"Why not stay, Longarm? I have no neighbors. There would be no one to notice your horse."

He smiled. "Thank you, but I think it would be simpler if I returned to my hotel room. I want to get an early start out to the J Bar tomorrow. And I want to check on Tim Landon before I go. I'm worried about him."

"All right," she said, getting to her feet. "I mustn't be greedy."

"No," he said, as she walked into his arms. "You mustn't."

A furious, embittered Pete Murchison returned that night from the town council meeting and headed for the bunkhouse. Making no effort to be quiet, he awakened Clint and told him to get dressed and meet him in his office in the main house.

A tired but wary Clint Swenson appeared fully dressed not long after and slouched into a chair by Murchison's desk. Murchison's long, lined face was weary, his white thatch of hair awry. He looked bewildered, frustrated, and angry, and Swenson knew that something bad had happened in that town council meeting.

Shaking his head in exasperation, Murchison said, "It's infuriating—insupportable!"

"What's that, Mr. Murchison?"

"You remember that big fellow in the Big Country—the one you said carted Tim Landon to the doc's?"

"Yeah?"

"Well, that son of a bitch owns the J Bar now."

Swenson leaned forward in his seat. "What in tarnation—"

"He's been a silent partner of Romero's all along," Murchison went on. "When he heard of the greaser's indictment for murder he came on up. He's already been to the land office, asking a lot of questions and checking on his deed."

"Who told you this?"

"Ned, one of the clerks in the office. He wasn't supposed to know about it, but I pay the little bastard well. He was at the town council meeting."

"So what do we do now?"

Murchison studied Swenson carefully for a moment, waiting. Then he sighed. "There's more, but you didn't catch it."

"I'm too tired for riddles, Mr. Murchison."

"Damn it! Don't you see? This man—his name is Custis Long—must be the one who bushwhacked Billy and killed Pete Bushnell. This is the son of a bitch who buried Romero and his wife. And now he's moving right into the J Bar. And, more than likely, he'll start up where Romero left off."

Swenson nodded slowly. "So he's the one. Sure as hell seems likely. And now he'll start scalping your range again."

"If this keeps up, I'll be ruined!"

"I'll ask you again, Mr. Murchison. What do you want me to do?"

"Burn him out! Take his cattle! Do what you have to do! I don't want that man to stay in this valley another week. Is that clear?"

"Clear enough," Swenson said.

"And one more thing. Borrman is through in this town. He's my biggest liability right now, and I want him out of here. Tomorrow wouldn't be soon enough. Tell him I don't want to see his face in the morning."

Swenson got to his feet. "You want us to move out tonight?"

"Yes. It's a long ride into that mountain valley. By tomorrow night I want to hear from you that the J Bar has been burned out."

"Mr. Murchison, you're asking for a little more than I can rightly ask anyone to do—without a sweetener."

"How much do you want?"

"One thousand."

"That's pretty steep, isn't it?"

"Do you want this Custis fellow burned out?"

"I'll get the money."

Swenson poked at Labeau impatiently. It took a while for him to get much of a response out of Labeau, so weary was the man. Swenson understood that completely. He was just as exhausted.

"What is it?" Labeau protested.

"Get up and meet me outside. Don't wake any of Murchison's hands, but get Slim and Borrman, too."

Mumbling unhappily, Labeau flicked his blanket off and sat up on the edge of his bunk, scratching his dark curls sleepily. Swenson didn't wait for any argument. He went outside and waited by the corral.

In a few minutes, the three men padded on bare feet out of the bunkhouse and caught sight of him. The three were wearing longjohns and, in the bright moonlight, they looked like comic apparitions as they picked their way across the yard.

"What the hell is this, Clint?" Borrman wanted to know. He was hugging himself to keep from shivering in the chill night air.

"Just got through talking to Murchison," Swenson replied.

"So what's he want?"

"He wants you out of this territory, for one thing," the sheriff said.

"Hell he does."

"Don't argue, Borrman. You fixed your wagon in the Big Country Saloon this afternoon."

"I'm not leaving," Borrman snarled.

"Play it smart. Lay low until feeling about what you done dies down some. You better hope the son of a bitch doesn't die."

"He had it coming."

"Who the hell is arguing with you? Just stay low at the canyon ranch until I get word to you," Swenson said firmly.

Borrman nodded sullenly.

Swenson looked at Labeau and Slim. In the moonlight, he could see Labeau's battered face, and Slim still had that dazed look about him on occasion that he couldn't seem to shake. "How'd you two like to get even with the son of a bitch who messed you up outside Romero's cabin?" he asked them.

"You mean you found the bastard?" Labeau asked, astonished.

71

"Murchison thinks he's that tall gent who stepped in when you started to work Landon over. You remember him, don't you?"

Labeau's eyes narrowed. "I sure as hell do. And, now that I think of it, he's a stranger in town."

"He was also Juan Romero's partner in the J Bar. He just got here, he says, and it looks like he's going to work the J Bar."

"He's the one," Slim growled. "I'd bet my life on it."

"Murchison wants him dead—and the J Bar burned out. You boys think you can handle that?"

Labeau took a deep breath and glanced at Slim. "That's a tall order. Murder and arson. And Slim and I been thinking of movin' on south. This country ain't no more to our liking. The women are pinched and milk-white and the land is too high and too cold. How much is in this for us?"

Swenson smiled. "I thought you might ask. A couple of hundred for both of you."

"Only a couple of hundred?"

"You finish this guy clean and it'll be five hundred apiece. And don't forget the satisfaction you'll be getting at the same time."

Labeau glanced at Slim. Slim nodded.

"All right," said Labeau. "Five hundred apiece, in silver—and also we get to choose the pick of the remuda when we start south. We got us some pretty fine horseflesh stashed in that canyon."

Swenson nodded. "We'll settle up the day after tomorrow at the canyon ranch. How's that?"

"Fine. You want us to pull out now?"

"Yes. I'll be in Cody, so no one can connect me

72

to any of this. Afterward you two can join Borrman at the ranch."

The three turned, made their way back across the yard, and disappeared into the bunkhouse. Swenson watched them go. Then he went back to the main house, where his saddled horse was waiting for him by the tie rail. As he swung into the saddle, he thought of what Labeau had said about leaving this high country for the warmth of the south.

It was too bad, he supposed, that neither of them was likely to make it south. The way Swenson had it figured, he'd be bringing their bodies back to Cody as the murderers of this fellow, Long. It would make him and Murchison look good for a change, and it would make himself a hell of a lot richer.

Yes, sir, he told himself as he put his horse through the gate, if he played his cards right, with Murchison's kid dead, he just might be able to chuck this badge, abandon the canyon ranch, and take over the Double M as ramrod.

Swenson began thinking of Cathy Murchison. She was a bit young for him, and she didn't seem to care for him much, but she was a lot of woman all the same. He liked the way she stood up to him and the boys in her father's office earlier that evening. And Tim Landon, no matter whether he lived or died, was no longer a rival.

As Clint Swenson rode on through the moonlit night, he found himself genuinely impressed by his prospects.

Chapter 6

That next morning, after looking in on Tim Landon, Longarm sent a telegram to Billy Vail in Denver. He informed the chief marshal of Juan's death, and added a brief description of Clint Swenson and his two side-kicks, along with a request that Vail see what he could find on them.

Though he had not been happy at Tim's condition, he put it behind him as he rode out to look over the J Bar ranch. It took him most of the morning to reach the valley. When he did, he was disturbed to see how little cattle was left on Juan's land. In a fruitless search for J Bar stock, he found himself eventually riding on Double M land.

He saw at once what Murchison had, and why the rancher was willing to go to any lengths to keep it and expand on it. Longarm found himself riding over land as broad and spacious as the ocean, the grass rolling off endlessly on either side in gentle swells that merged almost imperceptibly with the great blue hills shouldering distantly against the sky.

Grama grass, bluestem, even the tight, curly buffalo grass—he found it everywhere. It was so thick and lush that his horse's hooves made hardly a sound. Almost the only sound in his ears was the sweep of the wind as it rippled across the grass, constantly transforming its hue and its gentle contours.

There was water too, big springs welling up, sending icy rivulets across the fields, many of them feeding eventually into the same creek that flowed past the J Bar. Here, however, they coiled lazily through these fat hills toward a distant pine bluff clad with juniper and pine.

But where was the stock that should have been feeding on this magnificent grassland? Throughout his ride, Longarm had seen surprisingly few cattle. Even though he remembered what Mary had told him the night before—that Murchison was losing cattle to rustlers—Longarm was still not prepared for the scarcity of Double M beef. Indeed, he saw now why the grass was so lush, so tall. The few groups of crossbred longhorn-Herefords he had come across were doing fine. They were almost staggering under the weight of their tallow. But they were few and far between. And there was no sign—none at all—of J Bar beef.

Whoever was picking this range clean was doing a thorough job of it.

Late that afternoon, back on J Bar land, he saw tracks paralleling a long, high bluff. Curious, he followed them into an arroyo that led into a small box canyon. Like everywhere else in this lush country, the floor of the canyon was carpeted with chest-high grama and bluestem.

In the far corner, close by a small stream, he found nearly thirty head of fat J Bar cattle. He was pleased enough to smile some until he realized how little of Juan's stock this small gather represented. As he drove his meager find out of the canyon toward the ranch, his anger returned. Longarm had no doubt that Juan's cattle had been deliberately driven into that box canyon to be picked up later. Their brands would be altered and they would be delivered to a buyer elsewhere.

Like the Big M, the J Bar was being cut down to size. For the first time Longarm understood the frustration that must be driving the Big Outfit's owner.

He caught sight of the black column of smoke just before he reached the creek. The smoke was pumping furiously into the sky. At almost the same time the smell of burning came to him. He spurred his horse through the cattle, scattering them, and crested a grassy knoll that gave him an unobstructed view of his cabin on the far side of the creek.

It was almost totally consumed by this time. The underbelly of the black plumes of smoke glowed a bright red. Even as Longarm put his horse down the other side of the knoll, he saw the barn explode into flames. He rode his horse furiously across the shallow creek and loped up the bank on the far side.

The shot came as he hit the flat just below the cabin. The bullet missed him but nicked his horse's right flank. The animal reeled wildly beneath him. Longarm fought to stay in the saddle as another shot tore his hat off his head. The chin strap sawed against his Adam's apple. Sidestepping and twisting, the horse swung Longarm out—too far out.

Pitching headlong out of the saddle, Longarm hit into the ground shoulder first, then felt himself being yanked along the ground by the pull of the reins he still clutched. He let go. The horse bolted back down the valley.

A third shot cut the grass by Longarm's head. He rolled quickly away, raised himself to one knee, stumbled, then dove back to the creek. As he reached the bank, a fourth slug plowed into the back of his right shoulder, slamming him head first down the embankment. He caught himself halfway, unholstered his .44, and flung himself back up the embankment, ignoring as best he could the mind-numbing pain hammering in his shoulder.

Peering over the top of the embankment, Longarm saw the two horsemen charging down the slope leading from the burning cabin. He recognized them both: Curly Labeau and Slim Ratch. Both men had their rifles out, and both were leaning over the necks of their horses. Longarm steadied his .44 and waited, praying that the hammering in his shoulder would not spoil his aim.

He waited until he could see the individual strands of Slim's stringy blond hair. Then he fired twice, aiming low, in hopes of stopping their horses, at least. But the hunk of lead in his shoulder made concentration almost impossible. Each shot went wide, and by this time the two riders were levering their Winchesters rapidly, firing as they came.

Their shots tore up the ground in front of Longarm. Ducking away, he shifted his weapon to his left hand. The two riders were pounding up the embankment toward him, filling the air with lead. As they thundered closer, Longarm rolled to one side and fired upward. A great dark shape stretched across the sky, and another followed after, as both riders crested the embankment, intent on riding him down.

But he had rolled away just in time.

He kept rolling and firing. The two riders continued on down the steep embankment and into the streambed. When they tried to pull up and turn in their saddles to use their rifles, Longarm steadied his left hand with his right, aimed carefully at Labeau, and fired.

Labeau swore, yanked his horse around, and started galloping downstream away from Longarm. Slim followed, throwing a few shots back at Longarm as he did. Longarm saw Labeau slump forward in his saddle. Before he could pitch from his horse, Slim leaned over and steadied him. The two men conversed for a moment. Labeau pulled himself together and the two riders splashed back across the stream and headed north up the valley.

His right shoulder still hammering violently, Longarm struggled to his feet and watched the two men gallop out of sight. Then he turned to look for his horse. The animal had been spooked badly enough to send him into the next county. Instead, his mount was standing in the middle of the flat below the creek, cropping the lush pasture. Longarm's luck was holding, it seemed.

As he got closer to the horse, he could see the crimson slash that had been left as the slug creased its flank. Longarm kept on and began to speak softly to the horse. The animal's head pumped up, its ears going flat, its nostrils flaring.

"Come on now," Longarm said gently.

The horse backed up and Longarm forced a smile into his voice as he reached out for the reins with his left hand. "Easy, now. Easy."

The horse took another step backward, its flanks quivering. Longarm lunged for the reins and managed to grab hold of them as the animal, thoroughly alarmed now, reared, its forelegs kicking out. Longarm hung on and dug his heels into the thick carpet of grass. The horse came down, snorting and shaking its head from side to side.

"Easy," Longarm called softly, wondering why his right arm didn't just fall off and be done with it.

The horse stood with all four legs locked stiffly, ears flickering, tail snapping. Without releasing his hold on the reins, Longarm reached out with his left hand and pulled himself into the saddle. Then he swung his right leg over into the stirrup.

By this time his right shoulder was on fire and his right arm felt like a useless, leaden appendage. All down his back a thick blotch of blood was hardening. The pain reminded him of a small furious animal gnawing away at the bone and muscle. It was not pleasant, but it was something he was going to have to ignore for now. Already, however, the loss of blood was beginning to tell. Cold sweat stood out on his forehead. And the fact that, despite his recent exertion, his teeth were beginning to chatter uncontrollably told him he had better start back to Cody without any further delay.

He clapped his heels to the horse's flanks and set out.

Clint Swenson levered a fresh cartridge into his Winchester as Labeau and Slim rode closer. He was perched on an outcropping of rock at least twenty feet above the trail leading through the pass.

Wedging the rifle stock into his shoulder, he sighted on the lead rider, Slim. His fingers sweated against the wood of the stock as he waited for Slim to get closer. Abruptly, Slim turned in his saddle and leaned quickly to one side to grab at Labeau riding beside him.

Swenson swore and lowered his rifle.

Something was wrong. Labeau was having a helluva rough time staying in his saddle. Swenson stood up, watched the two riders a moment longer, then turned and jumped down off the rock. Snatching up his horse's reins, he swung into his saddle.

The rifle was in its scabbard as he cut onto the trail a few yards farther on. Swinging around, he rode toward the two men. When they saw him approaching, Slim and Labeau pulled up. As Swenson got closer, he saw that Labeau was simply hanging on to his saddlehorn. The man's dark face had lost all its color, and his thin lips were tightly compressed. Slim had a sullen, defiant look, and Swenson expected the worst.

"Okay," he said, pulling up alongside Slim. "What went wrong?"

Labeau mumbled, "I got shot. Bad."

"I can see that, damn it. Where'd you get hit?"

"My back—low. The slug's sitting in my gut now. Jesus Christ, Clint, I think I'm finished."

"Nonsense! I'll take care of you. Now, what about that fellow Long?"

Slim spoke up then. "We burnt him out, barn and all. There ain't a stick left standing. The place went up like a stack of dry hay."

"What about Long, damn it?"

"We winged him."

"You mean he got away?"

"Not before we caught him one, Clint. We got him in the back somewhere and sent him tumbling. But if he lives, he can identify us. Looks like we got no choice now. First chance we get, we'd better move on south, like we planned."

"You mean you let Long get a good look at you?" the sheriff raged.

Slim nodded unhappily.

"Never mind the palaver," said Labeau weakly. "Just get me a doctor, Clint."

"You want me to go into Cody and bring Doc Fletcher out?"

"I'm hurt bad, Clint."

"So I should bring Fletcher out here to the canyon ranch. And of course he won't notice a thing, will he? He won't notice the corrals or anything. You know I can't do that, Labeau."

"Just get him, Clint. I need him."

Swenson shrugged wearily and appeared to relent. "All right," he said. "I'll get the old son of a bitch. Maybe he won't even notice the corrals and loading pens. We've got plenty of booze around. We might even be able to convince him to stay with us for a while."

Labeau nodded gratefully.

Slim seemed satisfied. "Curly and I will be waiting at the ranch, Clint. And hurry it up. Curly's hurt bad. We need to get that bullet out."

Swenson nodded, his face grim with resolve. He was cursing himself for not having squeezed the trigger a few moments before. If he had brought in these two draped over their saddles, he would at least have gained some credibility in Cody—whether Long lived or died. But he had let the opportunity pass.

Now Slim was concerned enough about Labeau's condition to give Clint trouble. Bad trouble. He was already giving him orders.

"I'll be back as soon as I can," Swenson told the two men, and clapped spurs to his horse.

He was well down the trail before he turned in his saddle and looked back. Labeau was riding slumped over the saddlehorn and Slim was reaching out to steady him as they rode. He watched them until they disappeared into the pass.

Turning back around in his saddle, his face was lit by a bleak smile. Labeau would be dead by morning. He would pay Slim off and send him packing. No sense in lathering himself about it. He could forget all about bringing the doctor.

The thing now was to cover his tracks—and find out just how good or bad a job those two had done on Custis Long.

Cody's main street was quiet. The saloons had all shut down by this time. The only light came from the full moon sailing high overhead. It was all Longarm needed as he guided his horse through the town.

He was thinking foolish thoughts by this time, his

mind fully of fuzzy, tail-chasing ideas. It was almost as if he were in the middle of a high lonesome, except that he hadn't had a drink lately. A puncher was suddenly expelled from a darkened saloon, but not quietly and not without a few well chosen epithets as he picked himself up off the boardwalk and, leaning on a post, carefully fitted his hat onto his head. Sending one last curse at the darkened saloon, he charged onto his horse and rode recklessly past Longarm out of town.

Longarm left the town behind him not long after. He clung to his horse the way a sailor would to the deck in a hurricane and realized at last why they called a saddle a hurricane deck. Only this horse of his wasn't bucking. He was walking along the moonlit road as calmly and peacefully as a well watered steer.

If he could reach Mary, and if she could bring the doctor to dig the lead out of his shoulder, then maybe he could keep that promise he had made to Juan. He had told his dying friend that he would get them all—every last one of them. Now he was having trouble just staying in his saddle.

He felt a bleak despair. The weight of his promise to Juan seemed like an added terrible burden. He became aware of the chill wind on his burning, sweat-streaked face, of the dizziness...and suddenly, as if by sorcery, he found himself in front of Mary's cabin.

He got off his horse faster than he had intended, but he managed to stay on his feet. The horse stood patiently as Longarm clung to the saddle with his left hand and waited for the universe to stop spinning. At last he took a deep breath and left his horse, heading for the low porch in front of the cabin. The window showed light.

Reaching the porch post, he pulled up and sucked in huge gulps of air. Sweat was standing out on his face and crawling down the middle of his back. He used his left hand to propel him past the post. Leaning heavily on the door, he knocked.

He was ready to collapse, but he didn't want to frighten Mary. He knocked a second time and tried to make it louder.

The door swung open and Longarm lurched into the cabin. He heard Mary's gasp, then felt her hands supporting him, guiding him toward the bedroom. Dimly, he felt himself falling onto the soft counterpane, then past it into nothingness.

Chapter 7

Longarm heard the sound of Mary's buggy and got to his feet. He had put fresh coffee on the stove, and its fragrance filled the small cabin. A moment later Mary burst in, saw him standing there, and grinned happily.

"You're up!" she cried.

He smiled back at her. "And washed, shaved, and fed. I put on some coffee."

She frowned. "Are you going somewhere?"

"I think it's about time. Don't you?"

She shrugged and closed the door. "I suppose."

"I don't want you to think I'm not grateful," he told her.

"Prove it," she said, moving toward him.

He hugged her to him with his left arm. His right arm was still sore. She helped him by leaning close and going up on tiptoe. He kissed her warmly.

"Mmm," she said, "you *are* better. Shouldn't we check out the rest of you?"

"I don't suppose it would hurt any. It should be a good test of Doc Fletcher's skills."

"And my skill as well," she said, swinging him gently around and marching him into the bedroom.

Mary undressed him very carefully as Longarm not so carefully picked his way to her through her dress, her corset, her chemise, and finally her bloomers. At last, as she giggled delightedly, they fell back onto the bed, clasped in each other's arms.

"You smell so clean," she murmured, dropping her hand to his crotch.

Rolling carefully onto her, he said, "You just smell good."

His knee gently thrust her thighs apart and he entered her easily, pleased at her sigh of delight; and soon he had proven to them both that Fletcher was one hell of a doctor.

Longarm's pot of coffee had boiled away by the time they returned to the kitchen. Mary made a new pot, produced some homemade doughnuts, and they sat down for a final chat before Longarm left.

"I have some news," Mary said, "about Clint Swenson and Cathy Murchison."

"Oh?"

"It seems Swenson was on hand when she rode into town yesterday. He took it upon himself to greet her. But she treated him so coldly that everyone around noticed. She was heard to accuse him of being responsible for Tim's injury—and, of course, he *is* responsible in the sense that he did nothing to prevent it."

"I should have acted sooner myself," Longarm said unhappily.

She reached out and took his hand to comfort him. "Anyway, it means that Murchison and his daughter are very likely thinking of dumping the sheriff. He certainly has become a liability—at least as much as Borrman. And if he does go, that'll be a real revolution. No one around here doubts that Murchison imported Swenson."

"Maybe Cathy is willing to dump Swenson, but that doesn't necessarily mean her father is willing to go along, does it?"

Mary smiled. "That woman has a way of getting what she wants from any man, her father included."

"Still no sign of Swenson's two sidekicks, Labeau and Slim?"

"None. And people are beginning to remark on that."

Longarm nodded grimly. "How's Tim?" he asked.

"The operation seems to have helped some, but he's still not too good. I am not encouraged," she said, obviously troubled.

"Damn."

He finished his second doughnut and cup of coffee and got to his feet. His right arm was in a sling and his shoulder was still tightly bandaged, but the soreness was not nearly so bad as it had been a few days ago. He had spent some time outside the cabin this afternoon with his .44, firing right-handed. His aim was not what it should have been, and he was a little slow drawing, but he saw no sense in staying holed up in Mary's cabin any longer.

Mary had brought him a telegram from Billy Vail the day before. The message had been brief. So far,

Vail had found nothing to send him on either Swenson or his two henchmen.

Mary left the cabin with him and stood by as he saddled up and mounted. He leaned down and took her hand in his. "Thanks, Mary. For everything."

"Thank you, Longarm. Be careful now. And come back soon."

"I promise."

Touching the brim of his hat to her, he put his horse in motion and headed for Cody.

Longarm put the glass of water down and leaned close to hear what Tim Landon said.

"Thanks," Tim whispered.

Landon did not open his eyes as he spoke, and once he had thanked Longarm, he slowly turned his head to the wall. Longarm watched him a moment longer, took a deep breath, and turned away from the cot.

Doc Fletcher was standing in the doorway, a cup of whiskey in his hand. He had been watching as Longarm gave Tim the water. Longarm left the room and joined the doctor in his office.

"Well, that's some improvement anyway," Fletcher said, his long, saturnine face smiling faintly. "At least now he can tell us when he's thirsty."

"You think he'll be all right?"

Fletcher finished the whiskey in his cup. "Head injuries are always tough to predict," the doctor replied gloomily. "But that flap of bone that was impinging on the meningeal sac has been taken care of, so we'll see."

Longarm nodded and looked back at the lawyer. Landon's entire head was swathed in bandages. Doc

Fletcher had operated on him the day before. Mary had assisted in the operation and described to Longarm what the doctor had done. While she had held the lantern, Fletcher had drilled into Landon's skull and cut away a portion of bone that was pressing on Fletcher's brain. But, like Mary, Longarm did not feel too encouraged by Tim's response so far. "What's the possibility of permanent damage, Doctor?" he asked.

The man took a deep breath. "I'm afraid it is considerable." He looked closely at Longarm. "Ever see anyone who was kicked by a mule?"

"Close to it. I remember a young fellow back in West Virginia. His father was a blacksmith, and one day a horse kicked him in the head. He was never much good after that. He loved birds. Said he could hear them even when they weren't singing." Longarm glanced back at Tim. "None of us laughed. He grew into a big strapping fellow, as big as his old man, but with the mind of a child."

"Well," Doc Fletcher said, looking shrewdly into the empty cup in his hand, "that's about what I meant." Looking away from Tim, he went on, "How's that shoulder of yours?"

"Sore."

"It should be. But you were very lucky. The slug hit the bone and stopped. I figure you were moving away from its trajectory when you were hit."

"That's right. I was running like hell."

"Too bad Tim didn't run."

There was a rap on the outer door, and then it was pushed open. Looking past the doctor, Longarm saw Cathy Murchison step into the waiting room.

Doc Fletcher hurried out to greet her. "What brings

you here, Cathy?" he asked. "You don't look sick at all—the very picture of health, in fact."

She looked from the doctor to Longarm, then back to Fletcher. "I came to see . . . about Tim. I was wondering how he was."

"A little better," the doctor replied. "As a matter of fact, he just spoke up a few minutes ago and asked Long, here, for a glass of water. We are both encouraged by this response to the operation."

"Operation?" she gasped.

The tall, gaunt physician bent his head in acknowledgment of her concern. "Yes, I'm afraid so. An operation. Seems Tim's skull was cracked well enough to cause internal pressure and bleeding."

Her face had paled at the doctor's account of Tim's injury, and for a moment Longarm felt a little sorry for her, but she recovered nicely. "Well, then, I am sure he will be all right now. Won't he?" she asked.

"We'll see."

"You mean you're not sure?"

The doctor turned his back on Cathy and walked through the open doorway to his desk, on top of which sat his bottle of whiskey. As he unstoppered it and poured a healthy dollop into a white cup, he glanced at Longarm. "Why don't you tell her?" he said wearily.

Longarm explained quickly to Cathy about the possibility of permanent brain damage. When he had finished, she seemed considerably subdued, her optimism of a moment before vanished completely. Without a word, she moved back to one of the wooden chairs against the wall and sat down.

"I *am* sorry," she said in a small voice. "If my words had anything to do with this . . ." She glanced into the room where Tim lay, then suddenly bent her face into her hands and began to cry softly.

Longarm started toward her, but the doctor waved him off with a shake of his head. He brought the cup of whiskey over to her and held it in front of her. "Here's some medicine for those tears, Cathy," he told her. "The best there is."

She looked up at him, tears streaming down her face. With the back of one hand, she wiped both cheeks, and with the other she took the cup. Smiling gratefully, she took a healthy belt of the doctor's prescription.

"Feel better?"

She compressed her lips and nodded bravely.

"Good. Then I guess you're in a fit condition to hear some more bad news."

Cathy frowned.

"You got any idea what happened to Mr. Custis Long here?" the doctor went on.

She shook her head, then glanced over at him, her eyes blazing suddenly. Speaking to him directly, she said, "I was hoping you had left the county."

"Might as well," Long replied. "I was burnt out."

"Burnt out? By whom?"

"Curly Labeau and Slim Ratch. You know them, don't you? They hang with that sheriff your father brought up here to keep the peace. *His* peace."

"I know nothing about it," she said fiercely, "but I can tell you this: I firmly approve. You're no better than that Mexican who murdered my brother. You've killed two men already."

"Miss Murchison, did Carlotta Romero kill your brother?"

She looked quickly away from Longarm. "I want

93

to go in and see Tim," she told the doctor.

He nodded and led her into the room where Tim was resting. Longarm watched her as she bent over Tim's cot and called his name softly. There was no response. She straightened unhappily, thanked the doctor, and left the room. Sweeping up her wide-brimmed hat from the chair where she had left it, she disappeared out the door.

In the sudden silence both men could hear her boot heels on the outside steps as she descended to the street. The doctor looked at Longarm, a faint smile on his face. "That's a lot of woman, Long. Tough. Wrongheaded, maybe. But when she comes and when she goes, you know she's been by."

Longarm nodded coldly. "I reckon you do at that."

He told the doctor he was going downstairs to the Big Country, bid him farewell, and left his office. Shouldering his way through the batwings a moment later, he walked across the sawdust-covered floor and bellied up to the bar.

He paid for a beer, then turned around and surveyed the dim place. He was pleased to see Clint Swenson pushing himself warily away from a poker game, his eyes riveted on Longarm. Smiling sardonically, Longarm tipped up the stein and drained it. Then he slammed it down on the bar and started toward Swenson.

Swenson got quickly to his feet, his eyes narrowing. Those close by him moved quickly and prudently to one side.

Pulling up in front of Swenson, Longarm said, "No need to get nervous, Sheriff. Just tell me where Slim and Labeau are holed up."

Swenson's eyes narrowed. "Why?"

"They burnt me out, then tried to bushwhack me. I figure you or Murchison put them up to it. Am I right?"

"You're crazy, Long. I had nothing to do with that."

"Just tell me where they are."

Swenson smiled. "They left last week."

"Both of them?"

Swenson hesitated for just an instant, then he nodded. "Sure. Both of them. They're halfway to Texas by now."

"You're a liar. I caught Labeau in the back with a slug. It was a solid hit, not a flesh wound. He had real trouble staying in his saddle. If he's halfway to Texas, someone's carrying him there in a pine box."

"Hell, Long, you asked me where they were and I told you. If you don't want to believe me, that's your problem."

Longarm looked at the sheriff. Clint Swenson had already told Longarm more than he realized. That slight hesitation earlier meant that both men were not gone. And Labeau would be the one still in the area. And if Labeau were still here, more than likely his sidekick was in the area as well.

"Sit back down and finish your poker game, Sheriff," Longarm told him. "Just don't try to bluff, that's all. You ain't worth a damn at it."

With an oath, Swenson swung around and stormed out of the saloon.

Longarm went back to the bar for another beer, then took it over to a corner table and sat down. He had some thinking to do. Somehow he had to find a way to track down Labeau and his sidekick. That meant he would have to keep an eye on the sheriff.

But as yet he had no authority. And already he had stayed longer than he had intended. Billy Vail's telegram had said nothing about his continued stay in Cody, but it had been terse, perhaps even a little impatient. Longarm had received enough telegrams from Vail over the years to be able to judge the marshal's state of mind from their contents.

He was still mulling this over when Doc Fletcher entered the saloon, caught sight of Longarm, and hurried over.

"Is it Tim?" Longarm asked, frowning suddenly.

The doctor nodded wearily. "He's gone."

"Sit down."

Fletcher slumped into a chair. "The blacksmith's building his coffin now. I hated to lose that man, Long, but I try to tell myself it is for the best. More than likely, if he had pulled through, he would have been little use to himself or anyone else."

"I call it murder, Doc."

"It's murder, all right. Borrman killed that man."

"And Curly Labeau."

The doctor's face looked terribly drawn, in sharp contrast to the hope that had shone in it earlier, when there was still the possibility that his operation might have succeeded. His eyes were bleak and empty. Longarm had considered the doctor a sardonic, detached observer of men's follies, certainly strong enough not to let a single man's death affect him very deeply. But obviously Longarm had been wrong.

Longarm realized now that each man this doctor lost, each instance of a futile and senseless death, left him diminished, a little more ragged, a step closer to despair. No wonder he drank so heavily. And no wonder it was so difficult for the man to get himself drunk.

Longarm glanced at Fletcher. "I never got to know Tim, Doc. But what little I saw of him made me like him. Just one thing puzzles me. How come Tim Landon was so sure Juan did not kill Jed Murchison?"

"I guess that was my doin', Long."

"How come?"

"I'm what passes for the county coroner in these parts. When Burnside was fitting Jed for his coffin, he discovered something and called me down."

"What was it?"

"Jed had taken a long fall off someplace pretty high and landed in water. Both legs and at least four ribs were broken. In addition, his lungs had water in them. Burnside discovered that when he rolled him over."

Longarm leaned closer. "Go on."

"Jed was not killed where he was found. He was killed someplace else, then dumped on Juan's land— an obvious attempt to frame Juan."

"And Tim found out?"

"I told him. Another thing: I always had the feeling that Juan was on to something about the rustling that was hurting Murchison so much."

"What did he know?"

"I never found out for sure."

"Too bad. I'm pretty sure now that if we could find out who's behind the rustling, it would mean a solution to the entire puzzle. It would tell us who killed Jed Murchison and why Juan was framed."

Fletcher nodded, then looked at Longarm. "Judge Kyle wants me to bring you over to his chambers right now, if you've got the time. I just got through telling him about Tim's death."

Longarm finished his beer and got to his feet. "I think I know what he has in mind. Let's go."

A moment later, as Longarm and the doctor were halfway across the street, Longarm heard the sudden, ominous clatter of hooves. Glancing to his right, he saw Clint Swenson aboard a powerful bay bearing down on them both. He was using his quirt on the bay and roweling it furiously as he kept his mount on a steady course directly for them.

A warning shout came from someone on the sidewalk behind them, but Longarm was already making his move. Reaching out, he flung the doctor violently ahead of him, then dove back the way he had come.

The ground shook and he felt a hoof brush the back of his head while the long shadow of the horse passed over his prostrate form. Dust enveloped him as the sound of hooves receded. Longarm scrambled to his feet, reaching under his frock coat for his .44, but he saw at once it was too late.

Sheriff Clint Swenson was well out of range by now, and both he and his horse were obscured by dust.

Holstering his weapon, Longarm helped the doctor to his feet and continued on across the street and up the stairs to the judge's office. Judge Kyle was waiting for them, the door to his chambers wide open. As soon as he saw Longarm and the doctor, he hurried out and escorted them inside.

Closing the door behind them, he hurried around behind his desk, pawed among the papers scattered over the green blotter, and fished out a telegram. Handing it to Longarm, he told him to read it.

Longarm took it, read it, then looked back at the

judge. "It says you've got the power to appoint a deputy U.S. marshal."

"And it is signed by the territorial governor."

"You want me for the job, do you?" Longarm asked.

"We've already discussed it, Long. I was led to understand that you would accept."

"I'll have to check with my chief, Billy Vail."

"I have already done so. I have his permission—and quite an endorsement of your abilities."

Longarm shrugged. "Then I'm your man, I guess."

"I understand you have your own badge already. Is there anything else you need?"

"Warrants—three of them. All of them for attempted murder. One for Clint Swenson, one for Curly Labeau, and another for Slim Ratch."

The judge frowned. "I am not sure I understand. You said Clint Swenson?"

Doc Fletcher spoke up then. "Clint has gone off his rocker, Judge. He tried to trample us under his horse just now."

"Were there witnesses?" the judge asked.

"Half the town."

"Labeau and Slim Ratch were the ones who burned me out and tried to bushwhack me," Longarm told the judge. "And it was Labeau who flung Tim to the floor."

"You'll have the warrants first thing tomorrow."

"Thank you, Judge."

"No, Longarm. Thank *you*."

Chapter 8

Murchison spun angrily on his daughter, his face livid.

"Well, what did you expect?" he shouted. "That man threatened all of us. He killed young Bushnell and Billy Lester. Of course I sent Swenson over there to burn him out!"

"And to bushwhack him?"

"No! That was not part of it, Cathy. Believe me."

Cathy slumped back onto the horsehair sofa. She felt suddenly drained. The sight of her father turning on her like an animal at bay saddened her.

He stood behind his desk now, pain and frustration etched starkly on his lined, weathered face. Not until this moment had she realized what the death of his son and the events that followed had done to her father. In these last few terrible weeks, her father had been reduced to an old man, his graying hair now completely white. An indomitable, fierce old man, to be sure, but an old man nonetheless. And during all this time, the only thing she had considered was her own grief.

"It's all right, Father," she said hopelessly. "I have no right to complain. Of course Long is dangerous. And I can see how you must have felt with him coming in and taking over where that Mex left off—the same thing all over again. Swenson could see that too. He would figure he didn't even have to ask. Like the Mex, he was in the Double M's way."

Her father winced. "Don't you see, Cathy? This is the only choice a man has if he wants to hold on to what he's built up. We're like cattle after a long winter with the wolves circling and getting closer. If we don't fight, we're licked. We've got to fight back anyway we know how."

"*Any* way?"

"Yes, damn it! Any way."

"And so we import killers like Clint Swenson and his bunch from Texas. We give him a badge and turn him loose."

The old man shrugged. Looking bleakly at his daughter, he nodded. "Yes, that's what we have to do."

"I'm sorry for us, Father," she said. She got to her feet and looked at him without rancor, sorry now that she had lashed out with such fury earlier.

"Jed is dead," she said softly. "Tim Landon is dying. And it is not over yet for either of us."

She turned and left the room.

Outside, she drank in the cool, clear, sunlit air and

102

felt an enormous relief to be out of the house and away from the conflict with her father. She had ridden in angrily, anxious only to confront him with what she had learned in Doc Fletcher's office. But now she felt only a need to saddle up again and ride—this time ranging over the Double M's holdings.

She wanted to experience once again the intoxicating sweep of their grasslands, to let the sharp scent of sage cloud her senses, to feel the soft thud of hooves on thick, luxuriant turf as she rode. What she craved was tangible proof that this land she loved was still there, still worth the blood and the heartache it was costing them.

As she started for the barn, she caught sight of Clint Swenson riding in. Eager to have as little as possible to do with the man, she hurried across the compound and into the stable.

"Andy," she said softly to the old hostler, "saddle my horse."

Murchison was waiting for Clint on the porch. As Swenson dropped his reins over the hitch rail and mounted the steps, Murchison nodded coldly to the sheriff.

Clint came to a halt in front of Murchison, swept off his hat, and mopped his brow with his bandanna.

"Well," Murchison said coldly. "What is it?"

"You gonna make me stand out here?" Clint asked.

Murchison turned and led the way into the house. "Come inside, then."

Clint followed the big man into his study and went at once to the leather couch, slouching wearily into it.

Murchison stopped in front of his desk and fixed Clint with a cold, almost hostile gaze. "Why are you here?"

"I got news."

"Bad news, I take it."

"I ain't the sheriff no more. Custis Long—that fellow I sent Labeau and Slim to burn out—is the new sheriff."

"I saw that coming."

"So did I. But there's one thing neither of us saw."

"And what's that?"

"Long is a deputy U.S. marshal—has been all along."

Murchison sagged, then went behind his desk and sat down heavily. "My God! Are you certain of this?"

"I heard it in the Big Country from one of the council members. He told me just before Long himself walked in. And, sure enough, the big son of a bitch acted pretty damn sure of himself. Asked me about Labeau and Slim, and made a nasty crack about you."

"He wasn't very easy on Cathy, either," Murchison added bleakly. "She ran into him in the doc's office."

"When he first got here, Long wasn't in no official capacity. He just came up when he heard Romero was in trouble. But he's showin' a badge now. Kyle just got the authorization from the governor to appoint him. The telegram came this morning."

Murchison fixed Clint with a baleful stare. "And your two men weren't satisfied with burning him out. They tried to kill him."

Clint shrugged. "Aw, hell, Pete. They just got carried away, looks like."

"Damnation, Clint! They were acting on orders from you."

"I got more news," Clint said, without bothering to contradict Murchison. "You want to hear it?"

"I can't wait."

"I tried to run down Long when I rode out."

"Tried? You mean you botched it?"

Clint nodded. Murchison just looked at him.

"And there's more," Swenson continued.

"I'm waiting."

"Tim Landon is dead."

Murchison said nothing for what seemed like a full minute. He just went pale and sat there. When his color returned, he shook his head wearily. "I did not want Tim's death, Clint."

"It wasn't me who did it. It was Borrman."

"You should have stopped him. Instead you let Slim put in his two cents. And Labeau."

"Tim Landon was our enemy. *Your* enemy, Pete!"

"And now he is dead. His death points a finger at the Big Outfit, and that accusing finger says that we kill our enemies even when they work within the law. The death of that Mex was something else. He murdered my son. I'll even stand still for the death of his woman. But not for Tim Landon. I can't abide that, Clint, and neither can Cathy."

"Don't get your balls in an uproar. All we have to do is lay low for a while. It'll blow over. You'll see."

"Maybe it'll blow over if you pull out."

"Hell, Pete, there ain't no need for that. I like it up here."

"Look at it this way. The Mex is dead. We've cleaned the range of those other nesters and ranchers who were rustling our stock. You are no longer needed. Your job is done. It's time for you to leave these parts—and the sooner the better."

"I wish you'd think this over," Swenson said.

"I already have." Murchison got to his feet. "As long as you and your Texans stay on, I'll have trouble from this deputy U.S. marshal. Bad trouble. So get on your horse, Clint, and make tracks."

Clint saw that it was useless to argue any further. He felt like a schoolboy being dismissed by his schoolmaster, and he didn't much like the feeling. But he swallowed his anger and got to his feet.

It was not only anger he felt, but disappointment as well. With Jed gone and this new marshal on the prod, he had seen himself as Murchison's only recourse. This spread needed a ramrod, and he could be it. The thought had filled him with some hope as he rode out here.

Murchison got to his feet also, his manner softening. "I am not an unfair man, Clint—not to those who serve me loyally. And I must admit that you have done so. You will not be returning to Texas empty-handed."

As Murchison walked over to the huge safe in the corner, Clint watched intently. Murchison yanked the handle down and pulled open the heavy door. Clint could see the bulging sacks of gold and silver on the first and second shelves, the neat stacks of bills and coins on the others.

Murchison took out some bills and closed the safe. He counted out the money into Clint's hand.

"I think you'll agree, Clint, that this is more than generous. There's a thousand dollars here for each of your boys, and a good bonus for yourself."

"Thanks, Pete," Clint said, hastily counting the bills, then stuffing them into his pocket. "I'm sure they'll be satisfied."

"And you?"

"I wanted to stay, Pete. You know that."

"I'm sorry, Clint, but my decision is final."

With a shrug, Clint reached back to the sofa for his hat and slapped it on. "If that new deputy marshal ties a can to your tail, don't come running to me. I'll be where the sun is warm and the grass tall. And that's where I aim to stay."

"Fair enough."

Swenson touched his hatbrim in salute, turned, and strode from the room.

A moment later, as he approached his horse at the tie rail, he saw Cathy Murchison cutting across the back pasture and heading into the hills. She was astride her favorite mount.

For just a moment the thought of her and that safe full of money in Murchison's office came together. Startled at his own audacity, he thrust the idea from his mind. It would never work.

Even so, as he stepped wearily into his saddle, he could not entirely forget it. He glanced in her direction one more time, then swore softly to himself.

What the hell, he thought, as he swung his horse around to follow her.

Longarm was aware since first Mary had mentioned it to him that if he wanted to arrive at some understanding of what was going on in this valley, he would have to find out who was rustling the Big Outfit's cattle.

Had the Double M not been losing cattle at the rate it had, Murchison would not have been so wild to get rid of the other ranchers. And whoever killed Murchison's son and framed Juan for his murder must have been doing the rustling as well.

Sitting his horse now above the charred remains of the J Bar, Longarm thought over all this. Labeau and Slim had disappeared, as had Clint Swenson. Perhaps the three of them had already gone south. Maybe he should go after them, but he could not escape the fact that unless he found out who was sweeping these lush ranges clean, he would not be carrying out the task Judge Kyle had set for him. Cody and the surrounding county would remain in turmoil until he found the culprit. He would have to keep to this high country, then, until he did.

It was for this reason that he had posted himself on this ridge. Feeding contentedly in the flat below him was a small herd of close to twenty head. They were J Bar stock—all that remained of Juan's herd, as far as Longarm could tell. Drovers had herded them together and left them there. Like that other gather of J Bar beef he had found in the box canyon, these cattle had been rounded up preparatory to moving them on. Whoever was behind the rustling was obviously responsible for this gather below him.

And Longarm was waiting for him—or them—to show. He would wait all night, if necessary, and all the next day, if that was what it took.

Abruptly, he heard what he had been listening for— the distant bawling of cattle. Coming alert at once, he tipped his head slightly as the shrill whistles of the drovers floated up to him. The sound was coming from a distant stand of cottonwoods beyond the flat.

In a moment the beef left the timber, spilling out across the flat just below the burnt-out ranch. Then came the cowboys. There were two of them. Longarm did not recognize them. For a moment he had hoped they would turn out to be the missing Slim and Labeau.

This second herd was driven into the other gather waiting for them. Then the entire herd, now numbering close to fifty head, drove on past the remains of the J Bar and kept on up the valley. Longarm was about to move out after them, to follow at a discreet distance, when he saw another rider leaving the cottonwoods.

There was no mistaking this one. It was Cathy Murchison, riding a magnificent horse. A striking figure in her black riding costume, she was obviously keeping well back of the herd.

There were two possible explanations, Longarm realized. She could be the one behind the rustling, keeping tabs on her cohorts. Or, like him, she was doing what she could to find out who was combing the Big Outfit's ranges clean.

Longarm did not much like Cathy Murchison, but he respected her. He felt sure she could not be behind the rustling of her own or others' stock. Like him, then, she was trying to find out who was behind this business.

After waiting until she had ridden on past him up the valley, he put his horse down the steep slope and followed after her.

A mile past the J Bar boundaries, the trail left the banks of the stream and began a sharp climb to a high ridge paralleling the stream. Longarm found himself riding through steep land strewn with high rocks and boulders, some of them as big as houses.

High on the sheer mountain walls, Longarm caught sight of warped and stunted conifers that had found a purchase between the rocks as they competed grimly for survival. The wind became shrill as Longarm rode toward a jagged rampart of rock that towered ominously ahead of him. Passing under it, he felt dwarfed and not a little intimidated by this immense overhang of white rock.

Far below him on his right, the creek slashed its way through the narrow gorge. Ahead of him the trail was clear and well worn. He noted the pulverized rock where the feet of many cattle had passed. In places where the trail narrowed and where the beef had been hazed into pinching defiles, he could see tufts of their hair wedged in the rock cracks.

The sound of roaring water came to him more clearly as his mount tugged still higher. Soon he had been lifted into the chill land of the snowfields. Following the trail around a massive slab of rock, he found that the stream was flowing back beside the trail again, tumbling noisily through a narrow arroyo. He kept going and soon was riding across a grassy shelf bordering a small, icy lake fed by a large snowfield on the far side of the shelfland.

The trail worn across this level stretch was as broad and as clearly defined as the wagon road into Cody. It led clearly around the perimeter of the lake toward a stunted clump of cedars. Beyond the trees he saw the trail, broader now, coiling out of sight below the tableland as it followed a second stream leading from the lake.

Riding across the flat, Longarm saw the remains of many campfires along the shores of the lake, and realized he had found a pass that led through this mountain rampart. It was here that those men driving their rustled cattle through the pass rested up or sometimes slept through the night.

Longarm was almost to the cedars when he heard the sound of cattle bawling. The drovers must have pulled up. Swiftly, he dismounted and led his mount into some timber beside the trail. Tying up his horse, he drifted cautiously through the cedars. When he heard Cathy Murchison's angry voice, he pulled up, then moved stealthily closer.

Through the trees he glimpsed Cathy confronting the two drovers. The herd was beyond them.

"Didn't know it was you following us, Miss Cathy," said one of the drovers. He was past fifty, his sunken face as wrinkled as an old apple, and there was a gun in his hand.

His companion, a much younger man, seemed as nervous as he was. A frail, wiry fellow, he had light blue eyes, a receding chin, and a freckled forehead. He too had a gun in his hand.

What had happened was obvious: these were Double M hands. When they realized Cathy was trailing them, they had doubled back to trap her.

"Put down that gun, Smoke!" Cathy snapped to the older one. "You too, Toby!" Her voice was harsh with contempt.

"Can't do that, Miss Cathy," Smoke said unhappily. "Guess you're our prisoner now."

"Prisoner! You must be insane! I demand you tell me what you are doing with Double M cattle."

"Them ain't Double M cattle, Miss Cathy," Toby broke in quickly. "No, ma'am. Them's J Bar cattle. We found them grazin' near the J Bar. That new owner of the J Bar, he ain't shown for close to a week, so we figgered he got his fill of this country and lit out. So we just sort of took them."

His voice trailed off unhappily as he realized the hole he was digging for himself. He looked to Smoke for help.

"Yes, Smoke," said Cathy, her voice scathing. "And just where *were* you taking this beef? This trail is well worn, I noticed. This is not the first time you men have negotiated it with other ranchers' cattle, I'm sure."

Smoke took a deep breath. "I guess you got us dead to rights, Miss Cathy. We been rustlin' some cattle. And when we saw this J Bar stock, we just figured to rustle us some more, that's all."

"It ain't only us," Toby broke in hastily. "We ain't the ones behind it, Miss Cathy."

Longarm was about ready to unholster his .44 and disarm the two cowpokes when he felt rather than heard someone behind him. He began to turn, but he was too late as an oak tree crashed down onto his skull.

Chapter 9

As he sank to the ground, Longarm heard Cathy Murchison's scream. He tried to move, to fight back at the hands that dragged him from the cedars, but he was as helpless as a babe.

Someone was bending over him. Through slitted eyes he saw the face of Clint Swenson. Swenson might have been peering down at a bug he had just sent scurrying out from under a rock.

As if from a great distance, he heard Swenson tell Cathy to stop screaming. Ignoring her continued protest, Swenson and the two cowpokes began to drag Longarm across the ground. Cathy refused to be quiet, and Longarm heard the sharp, cruel sound of a palm smashing across her cheek. No further protest came from her.

Swenson spoke up from behind Longarm. "Throw him off here."

"Just like Jed, huh?" said Smoke.

"Shut up, damn you!"

Longarm tried to struggle free of the one who had him by the shoulders. He felt strength flowing back into his muscles.

"He's coming around!" Toby cried.

"Push him, damn it!" cried Swenson.

A hard, driving boot caught Longarm in the side. He felt himself begin to roll, then fall. He came down on his back with numbing force. His injured right shoulder sent a dagger of pain coursing through his neck and side. Clutching feebly at the jagged croppings of rock and the roots of scrub pine that poked out from the mountainside, he tried desperately to prevent himself from falling any further. But his punishing, tumbling descent was broken only for an instant as he found himself falling through space.

The icy waters of the creek closed over him, and the shuddering cold shocked him to complete consciousness. He struggled to the surface. As the swift current caught him up and swept him along, he managed a quick glance up at the trail overhead. He saw nothing as the beetling line of the ridge vanished from his line of vision.

The powerful current sucked him along, pulling him still more rapidly. Gasping for air, he slammed against a boulder and clung to it until the rapid current plucked him off and swept him on through a narrow defile. Reaching up, he caught hold of an overhanging shelf

114

and began to pull himself out of the swift stream. A faint rifle shot came from above him and a portion of the rock splintered into tiny shards. Another round followed the first. The whine of its ricochet filled the narrow passage.

He dropped back into the swift current, allowing the water to carry him on through. At once he found himself in much swifter water, then plunging through roaring rapids, dropping along with the water, skimming over rocks, occasionally slamming into them with numbing force. When he tried to regain some control, he found himself unable to muster the strength. Ahead of him he saw a patch of smooth, glassy water—and beyond it, nothing.

The roar of the cataract came dimly from below him an instant before he plunged headlong over the edge. Knifing into the churning pool at the foot of the waterfall, he found the cold paralyzing this time. A swift undertow caught him and dragged him still deeper into the icy depths. At last the churning and buffeting ceased. But the bone-numbing cold seemed to have sapped him of all strength. He made no effort to reach the surface as he began drifting down, down, away from the light, turning lazily, like something finished.

Or something dead.

The thought startled him. He began to pull toward the light. The pain in his oxygen-starved lungs was excruciating as he struggled to pull himself toward the surface gleaming remote and unattainable above him. Then he broke through. Behind him the cataract was still pounding into the pool, a mist rising like smoke into the air. He reached out for a slick ledge, grasped it, and pulled himself up onto it.

Shivering convulsively, he took deep lungfuls of air, and looked up with gratitude at a sky no longer quivering just out of reach.

It was pitch dark by the time Clint, his mind racing, returned from the loading pens and entered the ranch house kitchen. He found Smoke and Toby sitting at the table with Borrman and Slim Ratch. Borrman and Slim were playing cards, but the two punchers were just sitting there with tin cups of whiskey in their fists. They looked up apprehensively as Clint closed the door behind him.

"As I understand it," Clint said, looking squarely at the two punchers, "you two just took it into your heads to rustle what was left of the J Bar's cattle. That right?"

The two men nodded guiltily, like naughty boys caught behind the barn with their pants down.

"I'm going to give you both some advice, and you'd better take it. Like the rest of us, you've run out your string around these parts. Whatever gear you might have left at the Double M, go back and get it. Give Murchison your notice if you want. But then you ride, and keep on riding. Now go out and find some fresh mounts, then get back in here. I'll have something for you to take back to Murchison."

Smoke nodded quickly and downed his whiskey as Toby got hastily to his feet. In almost comic haste, the two punchers scrambled from the kitchen.

As soon as they were gone, Swenson turned to Borrman. "Is she tied up?"

Borrman nodded gloomily.

"She give you any trouble?"

"She bit some and hollered a mite. You mean you didn't hear her?"

"I was busy with the cattle." Clint turned to Slim. "Where's Labeau?"

"Hell, Clint, didn't you know? He died on the trail not long after we left you."

Clint nodded, pleased, though he did his best not to show it. "Good thing I couldn't get Doc Fletcher, then."

"Yeah," Slim said gloomily. "We dragged him off the trail into the canyon before we buried him."

Clint nodded and went over to the bedroom, opened the door, and stepped inside. Closing the door behind him, he turned to face Cathy Murchison and smiled.

By the light of the kerosene lamp on the dresser, he saw her clearly. She was lying on her side on top of the bed, her legs and arms tied securely behind her. Part of the bandanna Borrman had stuck into her mouth to shut her up was protruding from her mouth. Her eyes were wide and staring. As he approached, she began struggling to push herself away from him.

Ignoring her struggles, he bent to examine her. Borrman had done a good job. The ropes were a bit tight in places, but she would survive. He straightened and looked into her wide, furious eyes. She should have been terrified. Instead, Cathy Murchison was ready to spit in his eye if he gave her half the chance.

"Would you like some water?" he asked.

She hesitated. The fury in her eyes subsided somewhat. She nodded almost gratefully.

He returned to the kitchen, went over to the sink, and held a tin cup under the pump spout. He filled it to the brim with icy-cold water and returned to the bedroom. This time, as he approached her, she did not struggle away from him.

He stopped beside the bed and smiled down at her, the cup of cold spring water in his hand. Her large, dark eyes focused gratefully on the cup. Earlier that day those same eyes had snapped at him coldly and her words, filled with contempt and loathing, had stung him to his very soul.

He tipped the cup and let the water pour down onto her face and shoulders. Then he turned and left the room, closing the door firmly behind him.

Smoke and Toby were standing just inside the kitchen doorway waiting for him. Fishing a notebook and the stub of a pencil from his pocket, Clint sat down at the table and began to write. When he had finished, he folded the note carefully and handed it to Smoke. He knew that neither puncher could read or write.

"Give this to Murchison and I'll see to it that you get out of this county with your scalp. Mess up and you'll likely end up dancing a hemp jig."

Tucking the note into his vest pocket, Smoke said, "Don't worry, Clint. I'll make sure he gets it."

"See that you do. Now ride, both of you."

The two men turned and left the kitchen.

It was noon the next day when Longarm came suddenly alert. From the trail below the timber came the clash of iron on stone. Riders.

After an arduous, brutal climb the night before, he had regained the ridge. A search for the horse he had left in the timber proved fruitless, however, and he had used his waterproof tin of matches to build a fire and dry himself and his clothes out. It had taken most of the night to rid himself of the icy, bone-deep cold, and he had been too weak and his shoulder too sore, to do more than gather his strength during the morning, during which he had seen to his .44 and the derringer. He was afraid, however, that his watch was no longer a functioning timepiece.

He slipped through the timber until he could see the trail. Waiting a moment longer, he caught sight of the two riders. It was the two Double M punchers, Smoke and Toby.

Drawing his .44, he plunged the rest of the way through the timber, waited until the two men had ridden past, then stepped out onto the trail behind them.

"Hold it right there!" he told them.

They pulled up and flung their hands into the air.

"Dismount and keep your hands up. I don't care how difficult it is—just do it!"

Awkwardly, the two punchers dismounted, then turned to face him. The look on their faces was a pleasure for Longarm to see.

"My God, mister," said Smoke, "you must have nine lives."

"Never mind that. I need a mount, and you two are going to supply me with one. Now, where's Cathy Murchison?"

"At the canyon ranch."

"Where's that?"

"A ways from here."

"Look, mister," said Smoke, "we didn't have nothing to do with throwing you off that cliff. It was Clint Swenson."

"One of you two kicked me over. I remember that much."

Toby went pale.

"Please," said Smoke, "just let us give this note to Mr. Murchison and we'll clear out. No more rustling. We promise."

"What note?"

"Can I put my hand down?" Smoke asked.

Longarm nodded.

Smoke took a folded piece of notepaper from his shirt pocket. Moving gingerly toward Longarm, he handed it to him. Longarm took it, but did not read it.

"Both you men drop your weapons and move back."

They did as they were told. As they stepped back, Longarm strode forward and kicked both gunbelts off the trail. The two punchers winced at the sound of their guns clattering down the steep slope.

Then Longarm opened the note and read it.

Pete, I got your dauter. If you want to see her alive agen, bring me $50,000 to the J Bar ranch. Come alone. If I see anyone with you, I will not meet you and you will never see her alive agen.—Clint

Longarm whistled softly. Swenson had turned on his employer, and was holding Cathy for ransom. Longarm had an urge to find this canyon ranch on his own and free Cathy Murchison, but he realized that such heroics might well lead to her being injured or even worse. Clint Swenson and his men would not give her up without a fight. Besides, her father had a right to know what had happened to her. Since she had been gone all night, he must already be in some torment.

Longarm looked at the two punchers. "Either of you know what's in this note?"

They shrugged.

"Can't read," said Smoke.

"Me, neither," said Toby.

"Just as well, I guess." Pocketing the note, Longarm said, "I'll keep right behind you on your horse, Smoke. You and Toby will ride ahead of me on Toby's mount."

"Where are we headed?"

"The Double M."

Haggard from lack of sleep, Pete Murchison was standing on the porch of his house when Longarm rode into the Double M compound. As Longarm and the two punchers dismounted, the rest of the Big Outfit's riders drifted over from the bunkhouse and the barns. Smoke and Toby greeted them nervously.

Herding the two men ahead of him, Longarm mounted the steps and handed Murchison the note. Frowning the man took it. He read it and gasped. Then he read it a second time, his face flaming in outrage. Crumpling the note up, he flung it to one side.

"How did you happen to carry this note, Long?" he demanded.

"I took it from Smoke, here. I suggest you ask him about it."

"In here, you two," Murchison ordered. The cattleman looked bleakly at the rest of his hands. "Go on back to your bunkhouse, men. I'll send for you if I need you."

Grudgingly, the men turned and filed back across the compound. Murchison turned and entered his house,

Smoke and Toby following him, with Longarm bringing up the rear. As soon as they were all inside Murchison's office, he closed the door firmly behind them.

Immediately, he turned to Smoke. "Where's my daughter?" he demanded. "Where is Clint holding her?"

Smoke swallowed, looking miserably from Longarm to Murchison. "Say, would you mind telling me what was in that note?"

"It was a ransom note, damn you!" cried Murchison. "Clint's holding Cathy for ransom!"

Both men shuffled unhappily. Smoke looked away from Murchison's blazing eyes. "Jesus," he said unhappily.

"I'm sorry, Mr. Murchison," said Toby.

"Is that all you two have to say?" Murchison demanded.

The two men looked cautiously at Murchison and nodded.

Longarm spoke up then. "These two—along with Clint Swenson and his sidekicks, I am pretty sure—have been the jaspers cleaning your range."

Murchison looked as if Longarm had just kicked him in the belly. He glared with astonishment at his two trusted hands. They both shied back unhappily.

"What about Cathy?" Murchison demanded furiously. "If either of you has harmed a hair of her head, I'll—"

Smoke and Toby shook their heads frantically, desperate to placate the enraged cattleman. "She ain't been hurt none, Mr. Murchison!" cried Toby. "Ain't that a fact, Smoke?"

"It sure is! Yes, sir, Clint wouldn't hurt Miss Cathy none. He wouldn't dare!"

Wearily, Murchison turned from the two hapless punchers and looked at Longarm, obviously hoping for some explanation. "What can you tell me, Marshal? How did this happen?"

"Cathy caught sight of Smoke and Toby rustling what was left of the J Bar's stock, and she followed them a little too closely. I made the same mistake and took a long dive into the creek for my trouble. As near as I can gather, Swenson and his cohorts are holding her in a ranch somewhere in the mountains. I don't know where it is. Would you know of such a ranch?"

Murchison frowned. "In those mountains? Hell, I never heard of any ranch up there."

"It's on the other side," said Smoke helpfully. "Just follow the trail past the snowfield."

"It's hidden pretty good, though," said Toby.

Murchison turned to Longarm. "Since you're the law in these parts now, Marshal, it is your duty to take these two fools into Cody and lock them up. I'll deal with them later."

"I think we should see to your daughter first."

"Cathy is my problem. I'll handle this in my own way. And I will do nothing that might endanger her."

"You mean you're going to pay Swenson?"

"I mean I am going to do what this note demands. Is that clear?"

Longarm realized it would be futile to attempt to dissuade the man. He nodded without further comment.

Longarm did not take Smoke and Toby into Cody. Once out of sight of the Double M, he made them dismount, took their boots from them, and told them

123

to walk the rest of the way into Cody and present themselves to Judge Kyle. He told them that if they didn't do as he said, they would not soon get their boots back or a horse to ride.

Longarm spooked their mounts, then watched the two start walking toward Cody. After watching them for a while, he shook his head. There was no sight more pitiable than a cowboy afoot. As soon as the two men reached the horizon, Longarm turned his mount and, cutting west, heading toward the mountains— and the remains of the J Bar ranch.

Murchison guided his powerful dun across the creek where it coiled around a thick, screening stand of willows. The horse found itself struggling for a moment in the deep mud, then pulled itself up onto the bank. Murchison put the horse into the willows and dismounted. In the center of the grove, a long, half-rotted log sat like a bench in the midst of a park.

It was a place where Murchison had often come after the death of his wife. Here, in complete and blessed privacy, he could bellow out his fury at the gods that tormented him, or sit quietly and let the sound of the wind in the trees heal the loneliness that had left him raw at times.

He had come here after the death of Jed as well.

Nudging the log back with his powerful hands until he had exposed the dark, open soil beneath it, he took out a huge Bowie and dug a hole with swift, slashing strokes. With his bare hands, he clawed out the soil he had loosened. At last, satisfied that he had a hole large enough, he lifted the saddlebags from his horse, lugged them over to the hole, and dropped them into it.

Clawing the dirt back over the spot, he rolled the log back into place. He had tried to keep the loose dirt over the long, dark wound made by the rotting log and, for the most part, had succeeded. With the toes of his boots, he scattered what fresh soil was visible. At last, satisfied, he mounted up and rode out of the willows, splashed across the creek, and headed for the J Bar.

The sight of Juan Romero's burned-out cabin and outbuildings caused Murchison to feel guilty. For this deed, a just God was now punishing him. This gloomy thought was tucked quickly aside, however, the moment he caught sight of Borrman riding toward him from behind the barn's blackened ruin.

Guiding his dun through the creek, Murchison rode up the far bank, then reined in to await Borrman. He had been correct, he realized grimly, in figuring Borrman to be in this with the others. Capping his indignation at having to treat with this contemptible underling, Murchison sat his horse and waited for Borrman to pull up beside him.

"Howdy, Mr. Murchison," said the nervous former marshal. "See you got Clint's note."

"I did." Murchison looked quickly about at the blackened buildings. "Where's Cathy? Where's my daughter?"

"She's safe, Mr. Murchison, but she ain't here. You just hand over the money and we'll send your daughter back to you."

"Swine," said Murchison. "What makes you think I would hand over fifty thousand dollars on the strength of your word alone?"

Sweat broke out on Borrman's forehead. It was plain he had not been prepared for this eventuality.

Seeing his discomfiture, Murchison reached back swiftly and drew his big Colt.

"Unbuckle your gunbelt, Borrman, and let it drop."

Borrman did as he was told.

"Fine. Now take me to Cathy."

Borrman pulled his horse around and led the way along the creek, following a well worn trail that led past the cottonwoods. This then was the route the Double M's rustled cattle had been taking these many months, as Clint and his men robbed Murchison of his beef. That he had been so blind, so easily betrayed by those he had counted on, filled Murchison with a constricting, irrational fury. But he was determined not to lose control. At the moment, the only important thing was Cathy's safety. Nothing else mattered.

As the trail took Murchison higher into the foothills, he found himself wondering how the cattle could have been taken in this direction. Years before, while searching out the boundaries of his land, Murchison had scouted this trail and others like it that led into the mountains. Each time he had returned satisfied that there was no way to get his beef through these towering ramparts to the mining towns on the other side, since all the trails he had found petered out into box canyons, most of which were locked in almost year-round by ice and snow.

They were still moving along through some light timber, within sight of the creek below them, when Murchison heard the snort of a horse behind him. He swung around, his hand dropping to his Colt.

"Don't try it," said Clint Swenson.

Clint's weapon was aimed at Murchison's head, and the horse under him was standing steady. Murchison let his hand drop to his side.

"Unbuckle your gunbelt and let it drop," Clint told Murchison, an ironic smile on his face as he leaned over and handed back to Borrman the gunbelt Murchison had made Borrman drop back on the flat.

Murchison unbuckled his gunbelt and let it drop. "Where's Cathy?" he demanded.

"First things first, Pete. Where's the money?"

"I don't have it with me."

"Now, just what the hell is that supposed to mean?"

"Exactly what I said. You won't see any of it until I see Cathy safe."

"You think we're góing to let her go free before you come up with the cash?"

"The money's hidden where you won't find it. As soon as I see that Cathy is safe, I will draw you a map. I have buried the money on my land."

"How do I know you won't have me digging up half the Double M spread looking for it—map or no map?"

"Leave someone to guard Cathy and me. When you find the money, send word to have us released. I promise you that whoever you use for this purpose will not be charged."

"You expect me to believe that, do you?"

"Yes."

Clint considered a moment, then shrugged. "Guess I'll just have to trust you," he said, a shrewd light in his eyes. "Follow Borrman. I'll stay back to keep an eye on you."

As they continued on up the trail, Murchison contented himself with the thought that Swenson would not have agreed to his proposition if there was anything

127

wrong with Cathy. More than likely she was furious at this outrageous imposition, but at least, it appeared, she was alive and well.

Longarm sat his horse and watched the three riders disappear beyond the high timber.

He had seen it all: Murchison's encounter with Borrman and then with Clint Swenson. As Borrman led the way to the hidden ranch, Longarm was determined to stay back far enough not to get bushwhacked a second time. As he had hoped, he was going to be given another chance to beard all the lions in their den.

He flung away his cheroot, urged his mount out of the timber, and rode on up the trail.

Chapter 10

Mary could hardly believe her eyes. Two of the Big Outfit's ranch hands were walking across her back field on their way into Cody. Could both men possibly have been thrown at the same time? It hardly seemed likely.

On the other hand, it was difficult for Mary to conceive of anything short of a forced enlistment in hell that could make a working cowboy take to shank's mare. She let the kitchen window curtain drop and hurried from the house.

"Smoke! Toby!" she called.

They halted at her summons and turned to face her. They looked so woebegone that her heart went out to them at once.

"Hello, Miss Mary," they said, almost in unison.

"Goodness sakes! What are you two doing walking?"

"Marshal Long, ma'am," said Smoke unhappily.

"He spooked our horses," said Toby, "and told us to start walking."

Mary frowned. What on earth could have made Longarm do such a thing? Intrigued, she beckoned them into her cabin and held the door open for them as they trudged, footsore and weary, past her into the kitchen.

"How about some coffee?" she asked them.

Slumping into chairs by the deal table, they nodded to her gratefully.

As she plucked the coffee pot off the stove and headed for the kitchen pump, she said, "Now tell me all about it."

When, not long after, the men had finished the unhappy tale of their misguided adventures, Mary was a somber and troubled person. She understood perfectly what Longarm was about. He had been smart enough to know that Smoke and Toby would not get far on foot, and he had business elsewhere—desperate business.

She pushed aside her empty coffee cup and got briskly to her feet.

"I'll get the buggy out," she told them, "and take you both in to the judge. He's working late tonight. He'll have to lock you up, I'm afraid. We don't have a new town marshal yet."

"That's all right," said Smoke.

Toby smiled at her. "We can help you harness your team, Miss Mary."

"Thank you," she said, leading the way out of the kitchen.

Returning from Cody less than an hour later, Mary saddled her roan and rode west toward the mountains. There was a loaded Winchester in her saddle scabbard and a small Smith and Wesson stuck into her belt. She had been careful not to tell the judge or anyone else of her plans. Had she done so, they would have tried to stop her.

The thought of Cathy Murchison a prisoner of Clint Swenson and his Texans and of Longarm riding into that hornet's nest to free her had been enough to arouse Mary to action. Smoke and Toby had done a pretty fair job of telling her where Swenson's canyon ranch was located, and since she was already quite familiar with the country, she did not anticipate too much difficulty in finding it.

The truth was that she was sick of sitting behind a desk all day. She had been itching to get out, to sit a horse and ride once more.

Murchison had been awaiting his chance since night fell. And when they pulled up to water their horses, he was sure his opportunity had come.

He was almost certain that there was a rider on their tail. Before Borrman had ridden out from behind the ruined barn on J Bar land, Murchison had glimpsed a lone rider observing him from the ridge on the other side of the creek. Later, when Murchison had moved out with Borrman, he thought he had seen the rider leave the ridge and start after them.

He had no idea who the rider might be. Perhaps it was Long, even though the deputy should have been on his way into Cody with Smoke and Toby. Whoever it was, if Murchison could subdue Swenson and Borrman, this fellow would be able to help him free Cathy.

The horses had slaked their thirst. No longer watching Murchison closely, Swenson and Borrman bent to dip their hats into the icy stream. Swinging around, Murchison snatched Swenson's Winchester from the saddle scabbard on his horse.

The sudden movement alerted both men.

Borrman swore. Swenson said nothing as he lunged toward Murchison. With astonishing quickness, Swenson wrenched the rifle from Murchison's grasp. Disarmed, Murchison stepped back and tried to ward off Borrman and Swenson as the two fell upon him with savage thoroughness.

Borrman's fist buried itself in his midsection at about the same time that the barrel of Swenson's .45 crunched into the side of his head. Lights exploded deep within his skull. Murchison felt the ground slam up and strike him in the back. The night swirled crazily, drunkenly about him as Borrman started kicking him. Murchison tried to roll up into a ball to protect himself, but Borrman's lunging boot was skilled in finding vulnerable spots. A few blows landed on Murchison's kidney, and the pain that swarmed up through his body afterward made his teeth ache. If he could have cried out, he would have.

At last Swenson pulled the near-berserk Borrman off Murchison and bent to examine the cattleman. A thin trickle of blood was coming from the corner of Murchison's mouth. His eyes flickered feebly, but he could not seem to focus them.

Swenson nodded grimly and stood up. His head and shoulders lost in the darkness, he continued to look down at Murchison.

"I wish to hell he hadn't tried that," Swenson told

Borrman, "but there's no way we can let him go now."

"He ain't dead, is he?"

"He better not be. He's got to draw us that map, don't forget. Tie him onto his horse. We'll keep going. There ain't no moon, but if we take our time we can find the canyon all right."

Borrman nodded and bent close. Murchison felt the man's rough hands grab his wrists, then fling him over his shoulder. As Borrman swung him around and started for Murchison's horse, the cattleman passed out completely.

Cathy had heard the horses approaching the ranch house. A moment later came the harsh grate of Swenson's voice as he entered the kitchen. She breathed a sigh of relief. Slim Ratch had been coming in more often and staying longer each time. With each visit, the hunger in his eyes had grown more naked. She was positive that only her implacable hatred had kept him from handling her.

The bandanna had been taken out of her mouth, but her hands were still tied, and by this time she had lost most of the feeling in them, and her back, constantly arched as it was, ached horribly.

Now Swenson was back with the money and she would be freed.

Swenson's heavy footsteps approached the bedroom door. It swung open. His powerful figure filled the doorway for a moment, then he stepped back as Borrman carried someone past him into the room.

Her father!

"What have you done?" she gasped.

"It ain't us," said Swenson, approaching her. "It

was him. He got fancy. Wanted to see you before he gave us any money."

Borrman pulled up in front of the bed, her father still slung over his shoulder.

"Put him down on the bed beside Cathy," Swenson told Borrman. "Then untie her."

With careless brutality, Borrman dropped her father heavily onto the bed, causing it to jounce violently. The rope binding Cathy's wrists and ankles bit more deeply into the flesh. Cathy winced, but all she could think of was her father's pitiable condition as he lay face down on the bed beside her.

"What have you done to him?" she demanded of Murchison, close to tears.

"He's all right," Murchison replied roughly. "He'll maybe have a mean headache for a while, I reckon, but he ain't dead, if that's what's worrying you."

Borrman took out a knife and, moving around behind Cathy, began slicing through the ropes that had drawn her legs up sharply behind her. At once she straightened and felt a sudden, excruciating cramp in her left side from the exertion. She gasped. Borrman paid no attention as he reached roughly for her wrists and slashed up through the ropes binding them as well. Pulling her hands around in front of her, she began rubbing them frantically. As the circulation returned to her hands and feet, pins and needles swept down into them.

Ignoring this discomfort, she turned her father over onto his back. At once she saw the cruel welt on the side of his head and the dried blood on his mouth.

"You butcher!" she spat furiously as she turned to Swenson. "He was your friend! Haven't you already

134

done enough to him? Did you have to treat him like this as well?"

"None of this would have happened if he'd just brought the money, like my note said."

"Damn you! You call that an explanation?"

Swenson shrugged and took a step back. "I'll leave it to you to bring him around. He promised us a map to show us where he hid the ransom money. Just remember: the sooner we get the money, the sooner you and him can go back to the Double M."

He turned and left the room with Borrman.

As soon as they were gone, Cathy turned up the lamp and bent close to her father.

"Father! Can you hear me?"

Cathy saw a muscle on his face twitch. Then he opened his eyes and looked up at her. "I'm . . . I'm all right," he told her. "But don't tell them. If they know I'm conscious, they'll want me to draw that map for them."

Nodding, Cathy pushed herself off the bed and, with some difficulty, managed to stand upright. Then she turned and walked painfully over to the door. Pulling it open, she saw Swenson, Borrman, and Slim Ratch sitting at the kitchen table. They swung around to stare at her.

"He's awake now, is he?" Swenson said hopefully, getting to his feet.

"No," she said bitterly. "He's still unconscious. But I need towels and cold water to wash off his face and clean away the dried blood."

"We ain't got no towels," said Slim. "Use this." He ripped his bandanna from around his neck and threw it at her. "There's water at the sink."

She caught the bandanna and walked over to the sink. Dropping the bandanna into a bowl, she filled the bowl with water from the pump. As she started back to the bedroom with it, Swenson moved over and blocked her way. She looked up at him defiantly.

"You're in my way," she told him.

"Don't you let him play dead, Cathy. He's a tough old buffalo. If he don't come around soon, I'll just have to slap him awake myself—and that won't be so nice. You wash him off now good and proper and let us know soon's he comes around. There ain't no sense in you two tryin' to make this any tougher than it has to be."

She moved around him without comment. Once inside the bedroom, she leaned back against the door, closed it, and took a deep breath. Then she hurried across the room to her father. He stirred slightly as she sat down beside him.

"Just stay quiet," she whispered as she began wiping the dried blood and grime from his face and head. "They suspect you might already be awake."

He nodded slightly.

"There's something I must tell you," she said as she continued to dab at the welt on his temple.

"What is it?"

"It's about Jed."

His mouth became a grim line. "Go on."

"Swenson killed him."

Though she had done her best to prepare her father, he seemed dumbfounded. His eyes opened wide, and for a moment she thought he was going to cry out. Instinctively she placed a hand over his mouth.

At last, when it appeared her father had regained

his composure sufficiently, she removed her hand from his mouth. He looked at her bleakly for a long moment without speaking. Then he asked her to tell her how she had found out.

She told him then of being caught trailing Smoke and Toby and the way Swenson had evidently come up behind Long. It was when Swenson and Smoke were preparing to dump the marshal off the ledge into the creek that Smoke commented to Swenson that this was the way they had dealt with Jed.

"I heard it clearly," Cathy told her father. "Swenson was furious with Smoke for mentioning it, but I caught it at once. I just never let on I had heard."

"Long isn't dead," Murchison told her. "He's got Smoke and Toby in custody. He was the one who delivered Swenson's ransom note. He might even be on his way here now."

She stared incredulously at him. "Why, that's impossible! I saw them throw him off the ledge myself."

"He survived somehow, Cathy."

She frowned, attempting to recall that terrible business on the trail high above the creek. "Yes," she said thoughtfully. "Now that I recall, they did start to shoot at him *after* he had gone over. But then I heard them say he was swept into the rapids. I don't see how he could possibly have escaped."

"Well, he did."

She heard someone approaching the door. At once her father's eyes shut and she bent over his face with the wet bandanna. She was dabbing at his head when the door swung open and Swenson entered.

"He still out?"

She continued to work over her father. "Yes."

137

"Slim's goin' to bring in some food. You two stay in here the rest of the night. Let me know right away when he comes around."

She did not bother to respond as Swenson stepped back out of the room, pulling the door shut behind him.

The night before, darkness had come swiftly in the mountains beyond the snowfields, and Longarm had found the going difficult. If the trail was treacherous in daylight, it was downright dangerous in this gloom, hemmed in on all sides by towering walls of rock.

As Longarm had seen it, he had no choice but to dismount and find a spot to camp for the night.

But now Longarm was not so sure he had done the right thing as he found himself staring up at a solid wall of rock, the stream he had followed this far trickling through a narrow fissure in the wall. No rustled cattle had ever been driven through that wall, Longarm suspicioned.

Until mid-morning he had been following a trail pounded almost smooth by rustled cattle. Occasionally, imprinted on this trail, he had caught sight of the hoofprints of the three riders he was trailing. Then the walls of the canyon had closed in on the trail, leaving the streambed itself as the only feasible way to continue. Moving his horse out into the shallow stream, Longarm kept going. After a while, he came to a branch in the stream. Unable to decide which one to take, he had tried both.

He had found nothing going west, and now, after taking the southern branch, he had come upon a blank wall.

Pulling his mount around, he started back up the stream.

Regaining the fork in the stream, he dismounted and began to walk back along the western branch, his head down as he studied intently the gravel bed. The water was fast and crystal-clear at this point. Longarm was hoping for any sign at all. The tiniest impression in the sand would be sufficient to keep him going.

Gradually his eyes became alert to every unusual mark and disturbance in the stream bed, signs he had overlooked when first he had ridden through. Striated rock, tiny crushed fragments, and occasional hollows where cattle had foundered began to leap to his attention. Soon he was following the trail the J Bar's cattle had left as easily as if he were following their hoof-prints on dry land. That he had not done this earlier pained him somewhat as he pressed on through the swift, icy water.

Without warning, the signs of the herd's passage vanished. Longarm stopped and looked back upstream. The shoreline was crowded with stunted cedars and a thick, high grass, dun-colored and withered now. Behind the cedars stood a stand of lodgepole pines completely shielding the white rockface of the canyon wall behind them.

Still leading his horse, he pulled it around and slogged up onto the shore. He was about to start back up the stream again when he caught the gleam of something metallic in among the pines. He pushed his way past the bordering brush, reached down, and picked up a spur. The entire spur had been left behind: the heel band, spur strap, and rowel. The spur button had been torn off and the heel chain broken.

Dropping to one knee, Longarm examined the ground. The pine needles left little trace, but Longarm was sure he could make out two slight furrows in the ground, one of which ended in a small depression at the point where he had found the spur.

Its owner had been dragged past this spot, losing his spur in the process.

That meant the rider had been in pretty bad shape, and those dragging him had not noticed or cared that he had lost his spur. The spur's owner was no longer in any condition to care about such a loss. His working days were over. At once Longarm recalled Labeau. As Longarm had surmised, he had seriously wounded the man.

Longarm stood up and looked ahead of him, beyond the pines. It was in this direction that Labeau had been dragged. Pulling his mount after him, he walked through the pines, following the two slight furrows left by Labeau's heels. The tracks vanished completely. The solid floor of pine needles held no sign at all.

But Longarm kept going. He saw a tiny tuft of hair caught in a splintered sapling. Farther on, he found a broken and trampled fern. Then, tipping his head slightly, he heard just ahead of him the faint, dim sound of swift water. Increasing his pace, he found himself moving over a trembling shelf of rock. Beyond that he came to soft ground and the muddy tracks of countless hooves.

In a few more yards, the pine needles from the lodgepole stand had petered out completely, revealing once again the beaten, well worn trail taken by the J Bar cattle. He kept going. The roar of the stream he had heard earlier became much greater. Then he saw it ahead of him—a narrow, rushing stream cutting its way out from under the rock shelf over which he had just passed. Pulling up beside it, he watched it spill into a deep gully that cut sharply through the soft, red earth.

And beyond it, barely visible at the bottom of the heavily timbered slope, was the hidden canyon. The setup was damn near perfect. Rustled cattle could be hidden here and kept before shipment with little or no danger of discovery. Over the past months, Longarm had no doubt, the mining camps and towns on the western slope had proven to be a voracious market for the rustled cattle.

He glanced up through the pines. It was high noon. He would wait until dark before making his move. He slumped down with his back to a tree and lit a cheroot.

Chapter 11

Cathy moved to the window and peered out through the dirt-encrusted pane. She watched as Swenson, Borrman, and Slim went out to greet four visitors to the ranch—people she had never seen before.

For most of the afternoon, she and her father had been menaced periodically first by one, then by another of their captors. Swenson and the others seemed convinced that she and her father were deceiving them as to the seriousness of her father's head injury. Of the three, Slim Ratch took the most delight in his crude efforts to poke and shake her father into consciousness. Twice Cathy had had to pull him away from her father. Now, thank heaven, with the arrival of these four strangers, the attention of Swenson and his men had been diverted—at least momentarily—from Cathy and her father.

Greeting Swenson cheerfully, the four newcomers started toward the ranch house with him. Two of the strangers were roughly dressed range riders whom Cathy had never seen before. The other two were cut from a different cloth entirely. They seemed a good deal more prosperous, judging from the clothes they wore. One of them, the smallest, was wearing a bowler hat and was passing out cigars as he walked toward the house.

The men disappeared from sight, and a moment later Cathy heard them tramping into the kitchen. The scraping of chairs followed as they settled around the table. Moving to the door, she leaned her head against one of the panels and listened to the conversation.

At first she had hoped she might be able to attract the attention of these newcomers and persuade them to turn on Swenson and the others and release her and her father. But as she listened to the rough banter that passed between them, she realized how hopeless such a plan was.

The strangers were cattle buyers, come to bargain for the cattle that had been rustled by Smoke and Toby. The haggling did not last long, and it was obvious to Cathy that these men had done business together before, and regularly. The cattle buyers knew what they were purchasing, and as a result their offering price was shockingly low. Only a token argument was raised by Swenson, however, the price adjusted upwards slightly, and a bargain quickly struck.

As Cathy watched from the window, the cattle buyers went back outside to inspect the cattle they had just purchased. Slim was not with them, but Borrman kept pace, a jug of moonshine in his hand. He passed it among the buyers as they headed for the loading pens. They were making a party of it, Cathy realized miserably.

She returned to the bed and slumped down beside her father. He stirred and looked up at her, a question in his eyes.

"Shh," she said, leaning close. "Slim is still in the kitchen. Those riders were cattle buyers."

He nodded grimly.

For a long time the two sat silently as darkness seeped in through the windows. At length, Cathy stirred and leaned close to her father.

"Let me take a look in the kitchen," she whispered. "They've all been drinking. Slim's awful quiet in there. Maybe he's passed out."

He looked at her with sudden hope. "I'll go," he said.

"No," she insisted. "You're supposed to be still unconscious, don't forget. If Slim catches me, I'll just tell him I wanted some water."

Her father sighed and nodded. The bleakness returned to his eyes.

"Just be careful," he said. "Of all Swenson's men, I trust Slim the least."

Cathy patted her father reassuringly, then left the bed and approached the door softly. Lifting the latch, she pulled the door open. It creaked on its hinge. She froze and held her breath. But there was no outcry, no sound of any kind from the kitchen. She opened the door wider and peered into the kitchen.

Slim was sitting at the table with his back to her. His head was resting forward on his arms, and just beyond his head was a stoneware jug. Listening carefully, she was certain she could hear Slim's heavy breathing. As she had surmised, he had passed out.

His holster hung down over the seat of his chair, the butt of the gun facing her. It was the weapon she wanted. She glided into the kitchen and reached down for the revolver. Snatching it quickly, she yanked the heavy weapon from Slim's holster.

At once Slim sat up and turned around, a broad grin on his face. Cathy took a quick step back, brought up the weapon, and thumbed back the hammer. Aiming at Slim's grinning face, she took another step back. She was confused. Why was Slim smiling at her?

Slim got to his feet and advanced on her, still grinning.

"Stop right there, Slim," she cried. "I'll shoot! I'm warning you!"

Slim pulled up. "Go ahead," he told her happily. "Pull the trigger, Miss Cathy. Go on! Pull it!"

"You don't think I will?"

"Sure. I think you will."

She studied his face. It dawned on her then that he had come awake rather swiftly, that he had undoubtedly been expecting her to make just such a move. She caught the mockery in his face now, the pure insolence.

He brushed his long, greasy blond hair back off his face and smiled more broadly, revealing his uneven, yellowing teeth. They struck her as resembling fangs more than teeth. She took another step back, the heavy revolver trembling in her grasp.

As Slim reached out for the gun, Cathy closed her eyes and pulled the trigger. The hammer came down on an empty chamber. Before she could cock it again, Slim snatched the revolver from her.

Furious that he had tricked her, she rushed at him with hooked fingers, intent on raking her nails down his face. But Slim ducked almost casually to one side and brought an open hand around swiftly, catching her flush on the right cheek. The harsh blow yanked her head around violently, and Cathy felt herself slam back against the wall.

Before she could push away from it, Slim moved closer and slapped her twice—snapping her head first in one direction, then in another. The kitchen reeled about her as she sagged to the floor. She became dimly aware of Slim standing over her, a frightening, evil grin on his face. Then he reached down, grabbed the front of her dress, and hauled her roughly to her feet.

"I been lookin' forward to this, Miss Cathy," Slim spat, leaning his stubbled face close to hers. "Takin' you down a peg is gonna be a real pleasure!"

He flung her brutally back against the wall. The back of her head struck sharply. A sob broke from her throat.

It was at that moment that her father, uttering a cry like an enraged animal, flung himself from the bedroom. He caught Slim from behind with such suddenness and fury that Slim staggered back, but only for a moment.

Slim flung her father from him with almost casual ease. The cattleman staggered back awkwardly, struck the edge of the table, and slipped to the floor. As he tried to haul himself up, Slim brought his gun up and squeezed the trigger. The detonation deafened Cathy as a chunk of the table close to her father's hand disintegrated. Slim thumb-cocked the .45 and aimed again.

"Next time I'll come closer, Murchison," he told

her father. "I won't kill you—just wound you some."

Thoroughly cowed, Pete Murchison nodded and slumped into a seat by the table.

At that moment the sound of many hooves and the bleating of cattle filled the darkened yard outside the ranch house. The rustled beef were on their way to market. The house's frail foundations trembled as the bawling cattle pounded past it.

Cathy looked across the room at her father. He met her gaze, and she saw in his eyes a sudden hopelessness. The sound of the cattle moving out was an ominous reminder of their helpless state.

Slim caught the glance that passed between them and laughed.

"That's right. There goes the last of the J Bar cattle Smoke and Toby brought in—along with some Double M stock, Murchison. It sure was nice of you to pay us for rustlin' your cattle."

Cathy glared at Slim. "You won't get away with this!"

"Who's going to stop us?" he sneered.

The door opened and Swenson strode in, Borrman close on his heels. One glance told Swenson all he needed to know. When he saw both Cathy and her father in the kitchen, he grinned at Slim triumphantly.

"Looks like it worked, just like I said it would," he crowed.

Slim nodded, dropping his gun back into his holster. "Soon's I let on I was passed out, she left the bedroom and came after me."

"Didn't I hear a shot?" Swenson asked.

Slim indicated Cathy with a sharp nod. "This here hellcat really pulled the trigger on me. Good thing I

148

emptied that chamber. But it was like you said. Soon's I started slapping her around some, Murchison got better real fast."

Swenson paused beside Cathy's father. "Let's have it, Pete. Draw me that map."

"You can kill me, Swenson," the older man said, "but I'm not drawing you any map—not until I see Cathy ride out of here."

Swenson chuckled. "Hell, Pete, you ain't got no choice. We got ways of making you *want* to draw that map."

"Do what you want," her father snapped. "I will not help you."

"What about your daughter, Pete? You think she *wants* to let Slim here—and Borrman too—have their way with her?"

Her father glanced up at Swenson in sudden fury. "What are you threatening?" he demanded.

"You want me to draw you a picture?" He glanced over at Cathy and grinned. "Hell, I might take a turn at her myself."

"You . . . animal!" Cathy cried.

Swenson walked over to her. His smile was gone. "Now you listen to me," he told her. "You and your father been treatin' us like dirt. You were too good for us. We were just hired scum you brought up from Texas to do your dirty work for you. Remember what you said to me in Cody? You treated me like I didn't have no feelings."

"Feelings? *You?* You killed Jed! I heard what Smoke said! You *are* animals!"

"Sure," he said, seething. "Maybe we are animals. But even animals got feelings! And before we're

149

through with you, that's what we're goin' to turn you into—an animal." He grinned. "Just like us."

"Swenson!" her father cried. "Back off! Leave her alone, I say. I'll tell you where the money is. You don't even need a map."

Swenson spun about and hurried back to the table, his eyes gleaming in triumph.

"You know that willow grove near the creek back of the main house?" the old cattleman told Swenson brokenly. "The one in under the bluff. You've met me there once or twice."

Eyes narrowing in sudden comprehension, Swenson said, "Sure, I know the spot."

"The cash is in saddlebags, buried under the log in the clearing."

Swenson studied the cattleman shrewdly. "This the truth, Pete?"

Tears gleamed in the old man's eyes. "For God's sake, Clint," he pleaded, "take the saddlebags and ride out of this country. You've taken my son from me, shamed my daughter, and beaten me. What more do you want? Take the money and ride out."

The old man's plea seemed suddenly to shame Swenson. He swung around to face Slim. "Get them back into that room, and see they stay there."

Cathy hurried to her father's side and helped him back across the kitchen and into the bedroom. She felt only relief as the kitchen door was shut firmly behind them.

As soon as Cathy and her father disappeared into the bedroom, Swenson sat down at the table and reached for the jug. Slim and Borrman slumped down across from him.

"What're we gonna do with them two, Clint?" Borrman asked.

"We can't let them go. Thanks to Smoke, Murchison knows I killed his son. Murchison's still a big man in these parts, and they'll have half the territory on our heels."

Slim took the jug from Swenson and grinned. "You mean Murchison *was* a big man in these parts. I think maybe we took him down a peg tonight."

"That don't make no difference. Once he gets outa here, he'll get on his high horse pretty damn fast. You can count on it."

"So what do we do?" Borrman persisted.

Swenson looked at him. "You," he said, "will go outside right now and dig a hole. A big one—big enough to plant them both."

"Me? Where?"

"Find a spot, damn it."

"I'd rather not, Clint."

"I see. You'd rather pull the trigger on them, is that it?"

Borrman paled. "I didn't say that."

"Well, damn it, that's the choice you got."

"I'll dig it," Borrman said wearily. "I know a good spot off the trail, near where we buried Curly."

"See to it, then. Lefty and I will take care of Murchison and his girl—and afterward we'll see to this place."

"What do you mean?"

"We're going to burn it down. All of it. The barns, this house, and the pens. Before noon tomorrow we'll have our money and be on our way with no one the wiser."

"A lot of people are going to wonder what happened

to Murchison and his daughter."

"Let them. There ain't no law against that. They'll never find this canyon—not from the other side of the range, they won't. And there won't be nothing left standing here to connect us with their disappearance."

"What about Smoke and Toby?"

"They're gone, both of them. I told them to deliver that note to Murchison and ride out."

"I hope they did."

"We got nothin' to worry about. All the evidence is either going under the ground or up in smoke."

Borrman cleared his throat nervously. "Clint, are we going to have to kill them *both?* The girl too? I mean, I hate to think about it. Know what I mean?"

"Shut up," said Swenson, taking another swig from the jug. "Just shut up and stop thinking about it. All you got to do is dig a hole."

"Hell, Borrman," said Slim, grinning, "why don't you just figure you're out there digging us a new privy."

In spite of himself, Clint grinned at Slim. If you had to think about it at all, maybe that was the best way. You had to keep a sense of humor at a time like this.

Longarm moved silently through the darkness toward the valley floor below. The ranch buildings were huddled on the far side of the canyon, the faint yellow light of kerosene lamps glowing in the windows and brightening the raw ground about the ranch house.

Longarm paused. Someone was digging close by. He heard the sound of a spade slicing into the ground, its blade striking stone. The sound was coming from a spot to his right, not too far off the trail.

Longarm reached across under his frock coat and drew his .44. Crouching, he peered into the darkness and caught movement just behind a clump of juniper. Still keeping low, he cut through the brush toward the busy figure. The sound of digging grew louder with each step he took. Longarm kept moving and soon found himself directly behind the man.

Abruptly, the man stopped digging and straightened up. Pulling a bandanna from his pocket, he began mopping his face. At once Longarm saw who it was: Brad Borrman. And it was not a hole he was digging. It was a grave—a pretty damn big one.

"Just hold it right there, Borrman," Longarm said softly, stepping into view, his .44 trained on the man's ample gut.

Borrman's eyes bugged in terror. He stumbled back, away from the apparition which had materialized out of the moonless night.

"That's right," said Longarm quietly, stepping closer. "I'm not dead. Now, who's this grave for? It sure as hell is big enough."

Borrman shook off his terror. He saw at once that he was not dealing with a ghost. Snatching up the spade's handle, he brought it around in a vicious, sweeping arc. Longarm ducked just in time, losing his hat. He did not want to fire his gun. The shot would alert everyone in the canyon. Borrman obviously realized this as he brought the shovel around a second time.

Again Longarm ducked, but this time as Borrman followed through, he hurled himself at Borrman, catching him in the chest with his left shoulder, and drove him back. With a startled gasp, Borrman lost his balance and toppled into the open grave. Longarm jumped down beside him and with one swing of his gun barrel clubbed him senseless. Borrman's head snapped around, then lay still. Climbing out of the grave, Longarm retrieved his hat and looked down at the unconscious man.

He needed to keep the former town marshal out of action for a while, and he had no rope with which to tie him. Grabbing the shovel, he began to fill in the grave. He shoveled swiftly, and soon the only portion of Borrman that was not completely covered was the nose on his face. Tossing the shovel aside, Longarm moved back through the timber, then continued on down the trail to the ranch house.

Swenson and Slim were almost drunk. Pushing the jug from him, Swenson looked grimly across the table at Slim. "Reckon it's time."

Slim nodded, his eyes alight.

Swenson reached into his pocket and produced a pack of greasy playing cards.

"We gonna use your cards?" Slim asked, his eyes narrowing.

"Sure. You got any objections?"

Slim reached for the jug and hoisted it expertly over his right shoulder. He took a couple of hefty swallows, then slammed the jug back down onto the table. Grinning, he wiped his mouth with the back of his hand.

"What the hell difference does it make, Clint? You've already got me figured for the job."

"No, I ain't. I told you. We'll draw for it."

"Sure, Clint. Sure," Slim said sarcastically.

"I mean it, damn it!" As he spoke, Swenson slammed the deck down on the table between them.

"High card rings the bell," said Slim.

"Low card."

"I said high card, Clint. I called it."

"All right. Go ahead. Cut."

Slim cut the cards. Swenson put the deck back together and began to shuffle the cards. The sounds they made snapping together filled the quiet room. Murchison and Cathy were in the bedroom, trussed like turkeys ready for the oven. Slim had seen to that. As he had explained it to Swenson, this way they would hear someone enter the room behind them, hear the footsteps getting closer... and closer...

"You gonna shuffle them cards forever?" Slim wanted to know. "You'll wear them out."

"You're pretty damn anxious, ain't you?"

"Sure. Ain't you?"

Swenson shrugged and slapped the cards down on the table. "Go ahead. You first."

Slim cut the deck and held up his card. It was the ace of spades.

"No need for me to cut," said Swenson, feeling as if someone had just taken an enormous load off his shoulders. He was relieved, and that was a fact. Looking across the table, he was astonished to see that Slim was not a bit unhappy. Hell, the crazy son of a bitch was happy as a pig in shit.

"Looks like I get the brass ring," Slim said, snatching up the jug and grinning at Swenson.

"My God, Slim, you *want* to be the one pulls the trigger. You were afraid *I* was gonna get the high card!"

Slim leaned closer, his eyes glittering. "I hate that girl, Clint. And her old man. You're right. This will be a pleasure. Hell, Clint, how come you don't want to do the honors? I know that woman scorned you."

"I don't want to talk about it," Swenson said, shuddering involuntarily. "You won the right to pull the trigger. You won it fair and square. Some guys have all the luck."

Completely unaware of Swenson's sarcasm, Slim leaned back and beamed.

"Just tell me one thing," Clint went on.

"Sure, Clint."

"You gonna use a gun, or would you prefer to use your bare hands?"

Slim considered Swenson's question seriously. "Guess maybe I'll use my gun," he said. "Saw a guy strangled once—takes forever."

Swenson reached for the jug. "Well, go in there and do it, then. Borrman should be back any minute. And we got the barn and this place here to torch yet."

Slim pushed his chair back and got to his feet. Lifting his gun from its holster, he spun the cylinder to check the load, then moved toward the bedroom door.

Watching him, observing the demented gleam in Slim's eye as he reached the bedroom door, Swenson was more than ever convinced that he was right in going through with what he had planned.

They had already poured kerosene over the floors and walls of the barn, and a wagonload of hay saturated with kerosene and coal oil was waiting to be ignited and sent crashing against the ranch house. But it was not only the bodies of Murchison and his daughter he was planning to burn. He was going to feed Brad Borrman and Slim Ratch to those flames as well.

Swenson saw no reason at all why he should share that ransom money with a fool and a madman.

Chapter 12

Longarm eased himself over the windowsill and low-ered the sash. In the feeble light spread by the guttering kerosene lamp on the dresser, he had glimpsed from outside the trussed figures of Murchison and Cathy. As he turned to face them, he heard the sound of footsteps approaching the door leading from the kitchen.

Darting across the room, he flattened himself against the wall a second before the door swung open. A tall, slouching figure entered the room. It was Slim Ratch. Without closing the door, he started across the room toward the two trussed figures on the bed.

Stepping out from behind the door, Longarm saw a gun glinting in Slim's right hand. From the stealthy way in which he approached Murchison and Cathy, it was obvious what his intentions were. Longarm left the wall and eased himself across the floor, hoping to surprise Slim from behind.

As Slim lifted his weapon and took aim at the back of Murchison's skull, a floorboard creaked under Longarm's foot.

Slim spun about just as Longarm swung the barrel of his .44. Instead of coming down squarely on Slim's head, the gun barrel glanced off the side of it, ripping away a piece of Slim's left ear and crunching down upon his shoulder.

Groaning, Slim spun back to the wall, slamming into it heavily, his gun still clutched in his right hand. Raising it, he fired at Longarm, the slug singing past Longarm's ear and thudding into the wall behind him.

Moving in swiftly, Longarm knocked the weapon out of Slim's grasp with a single brutal swipe of his .44. Then, reaching over, he hauled the stunned Slim away from the wall and clubbed him a second time with his gun barrel. He caught him this time squarely on the side of the head, the force of the blow driving Slim back against the wall.

As Slim sagged to the floor, Swenson appeared in the doorway. Standing in the relative brightness of the kitchen, Swenson apparently was having difficulty seeing into the dim room.

"What's the matter, Slim?" he asked. "You having trouble?"

Longarm spun as Swenson drew his revolver and stepped into the bedroom, heading directly for Longarm. Swenson still did not recognize the lawman.

"What is it, Slim?" he demanded. "What's wrong?"

Ducking swiftly, Longarm crabbed sideways, his .44 trained on Swenson. "Drop that gun, Swenson."

The man froze.

"I said drop it," Longarm repeated.

Convulsively, Swenson shoved his gun hand forward and squeezed off a shot. Longarm ducked aside and returned Swenson's fire. In the darkened room, the twin gun flashes were enough to make Longarm glance aside. In that instant, Swenson spun about and vanished from the room. Scrambling after him, Longarm heard the outside door slam shut.

Continuing into the kitchen, he pushed the door open and was met by a fusillade from Swenson that splintered the door panels and ripped out portions of the doorjamb. Hastily pulling the door shut, Longarm ducked to one side. Swenson had a rifle now, and he was sending fire through the kitchen windows. Keeping his head low, Longarm ducked back toward the bedroom door.

At that moment Slim Ratch plunged out of the bedroom past him, heading for the kitchen door. The left side of his face and most of his long, blond hair was dark with blood. Longarm flung a shot at him, but Slim kept going and burst out the door.

"It's me, Clint!" Slim cried, racing toward the barn. "It's me! Don't shoot!"

The firing ceased as Slim disappeared into the darkness. Longarm turned and hurried back into the bedroom.

The two bound figures on the bed were struggling to free themselves. Longarm could imagine their terror. The sudden thunderclap of Longarm's and Slim's guns a moment before, amplified to a shuddering intensity by the walls and bare floor, must have turned their hearts to jelly.

161

Swiftly, he untied first Cathy's bonds, then her father's.

"I was right," Murchison said to Longarm. "It *was* you I saw tailing us."

"That's right. Took me a while to find this canyon, though."

"Where's Swenson—and Slim?" Cathy asked, rubbing her hands together to restore the circulation.

"Outside. They've got us pinned down in here, but I've taken care of Borrman, so it's just the two of them." He looked sharply at Murchison. "Can you use a gun?"

"Of course," Murchison snapped.

"Good." Longarm reached down, picked up Slim's revolver, and handed it to the cattleman. "Cover me from the window while I try to break out of here."

The man nodded grimly and hurried over to the window. As he crouched beside it, the fusillade from the barn opened up on the ranch house again. This time, rounds began pouring through the bedroom window as well.

Both Longarm and Cathy ducked low, then darted for the inside wall as Murchison began returning the fire. Leaving Cathy huddled in a corner, Longarm darted into the kitchen and opened the door a crack.

He saw gun flashes from beside the barn's open door. Peering carefully into the darkness, he thought he saw someone crouching beside a wagon piled high with hay. He was big enough to be Clint Swenson. Someone else was firing from the barn window. That would be Slim. Aiming carefully, Longarm squeezed off two quick shots at the figure crouched beside the wagon.

Longarm's only intent was to cause Swenson to duck back, giving Longarm a chance to dart out of the kitchen and encircle the barn. To his surprise, however, his fire caused the loaded wagon beside Swenson to explode into flames. With incredible speed, the flames enveloped the wagon, while tendrils of fire began to creep along the ground toward the barn as well. It became as bright as day in front of the barn. Longarm saw Swenson clearly, and he snapped off two quick shots at the man.

Swenson turned and darted out of sight behind the wagon.

A second later, the blazing wagon began to move toward the ranch house. Belatedly, Longarm started to push himself out through the open kitchen door, but was at once met by a withering fire from the barn window. He ducked back inside as the blazing wagon gained momentum and began an increasingly accelerating plunge toward the ranch house.

Slamming the door shut, Longarm hurried into the bedroom. Snatching Cathy by the arm, he turned to Murchison, who was still crouched by the window. The cattleman seemed mesmerized by the onrushing wagon of fire.

"Back! Get away from that side of the house!" Longarm called to him, pulling Cathy out of the corner and against the far wall.

Murchison roused himself and rushed across the room toward Longarm and his daughter. But he got no more than halfway when the blazing wagon struck. The entire house shook with the force of the collision. A portion of the wall near the kitchen collapsed inward and a sudden, blasting tongue of flame rolled across

163

the floor toward them. The bed vanished in an instant. Black, dense smoke enveloped the bedroom as the entire ranch house shuddered in the grip of the devouring fire.

"The window! Out the window!" Longarm shouted above the roaring fire. "The flames should hide us!"

Murchison nodded as Longarm, shielding his face with his forearm, led the way back to the window. Its frame had been shattered by the force of the collision, and the heat from the blazing wagon, now lodged securely between the floor and the ceiling, was hellish.

Murchison began knocking the glass out of the shattered sash with his gun barrel while Longarm took off his coat and placed it down over the sill to protect them as they climbed out. Holding her hand over her head to protect it from the searing heat, Cathy climbed out, then turned immediately to help her father clamber out after her.

Suddenly the wall between the kitchen and the bedroom went up in a ball of fire. Shying away from it, Longarm climbed out after Murchison and Cathy. The explosion had so stunned them that they were huddling like terrified children on the ground before the window. Longarm snatched his smoking coat off the windowsill and pulled it on.

"Get around behind the house!" he told them. "Those trees over there—hurry up! You're not safe here!"

Murchison nodded and pulled Cathy after him as he ran toward the pines. In a moment, the two had vanished into the timber. Longarm quickly reloaded his .44. Then, crouching low, he headed obliquely toward the barn, hoping to surprise Swenson and Slim.

By this time smoke was pouring out of the barn's windows and lofts. Longarm was less than ten yards from the barn door when four horses bolted out through it. They were too wild with fear to see him. Longarm dodged the first two, but the third caught him a glancing blow, knocking him to the ground. The fourth horse galloped straight over him, its hooves missing Longarm's head by inches.

As the horses passed, Longarm started to get to his feet. He was just in time to see Slim, astride a powerful dun, charge out of the barn, heading right for him. Crouching, Longarm waited until Slim was almost on him. Then he dodged to one side and leaped upward, hooking Slim's elbow. As the horse galloped past, Longarm pulled Slim from his saddle. Both men hit the ground with numbing force, Longarm landing on his injured shoulder and losing his revolver.

The sudden, acute spasm of pain momentarily immobilized Longarm. Slim took this opportunity to scramble swiftly back up onto his feet, his long blond hair partially burnt away, one side of his face still dark with dried blood. He was about to flee when he saw Longarm's difficulty. Sensing an advantage, he flung himself back down onto Longarm.

The two men struggled awkwardly until Longarm managed to roll over and pin Slim under him. He began to pound him with such a singleminded, murderous fury that he was actually driving Slim's head into the ground. But by this time his right shoulder was giving out, and he knew he could not continue for much longer. At that moment he caught sight of his .44. Snatching it up, he flung himself erect and aimed down carefully at Slim. He did not want to miss.

"No, you can't!" Slim cried. "That's murder!"

Longarm hesitated.

In that instant, Slim jumped to his feet and raced back to the barn. Cursing, Longarm raced after him. Catching him from behind, Longarm spun him around. Slim grabbed Longarm, and the two crashed to the floor. Slim landed on a patch of burning hay. Screeching in terror, Slim tried to break free of Longarm's grasp. Wrapping his good arm around Slim's neck, Longarm pressed Slim back down onto the blazing hay.

"You're going to fry, Slim!" Longarm cried.

But Slim was too terrified to be held. Twisting wildly, he leaped to his feet just in time to be struck on the back by a falling bundle of blazing hay. Screaming, he spun away from it and tumbled backward into a horse stall.

As Longarm started in after him, Slim emerged with a pitchfork held out in front of him. His face contorted, he lunged at Longarm. Flinging up his left hand to ward off the tines, he dove in under them and caught Slim in the midsection, driving him back.

At that moment a beam wrapped in flames plunged down out of the loft and crashed to the floor beside him. The heat from it was intense, but Longarm ignored it as he continued to drive Slim deeper into the barn.

It was too much for Slim, however. With a terrified shriek, he dropped the pitchfork and broke away from Longarm. He had taken no more than three steps toward the open barn door when another blazing beam crashed down from the loft, striking Slim a glancing blow that knocked him sideways into a wall of blazing hay. Instantly, Slim was enveloped in flames. A screaming, animated torch, he plunged blindly out into the night.

Shielding his eyes with his left arm, Longarm raced out after Slim. Catching up to him, he tripped him deliberately, then began rolling him over and over on the ground, heedless of his own blistering hands as he did so, and without even questioning his frantic effort to save a man he had wanted to kill only a few moments before.

From behind him came running footsteps. As he turned, Cathy shouldered him aside and flung a bucket of water onto the burning figure. Behind her came Murchison with another bucket of water. In a moment Slim was a sodden, smoking ruin. Longarm got to his feet and stood back, his eyes fixed on the whimpering, blackened figure writhing slowly on the ground. Slim's face was raw, his eyebrows gone along with most of his hair, his eyes staring sightlessly up at them as his blistered lips worked feebly. Longarm looked away.

"Will he live?" Cathy asked softly.

"He'll live," said her father, "more's the pity."

Longarm caught a sudden movement out of the corner of his eye. Turning, he saw Clint Swenson running from the darkness behind the blazing barn— running toward the dun Slim had ridden out of the barn. The horse had come to a halt a few hundred yards beyond the ranch.

Longarm tried to raise his Colt, but it was impossible. By this time his right shoulder was practically useless when it came to aiming and firing his revolver. Cursing, he watched Swenson vault into the saddle and ride off, heading back toward the trail leading from the canyon.

"Stop him!" Murchison groaned. "He's getting away!"

As the sound of Swenson's horse faded into the

night, Longarm turned wearily to Murchison. "He won't get far. Not in this territory. I promise you that."

"He knows where the ransom money is."

"You mean you didn't bring it when you came here? Maybe you better explain that."

When Murchison had, Longarm nodded. "Then I have a pretty damn good idea where to find Swenson—if I hurry."

Abruptly, a cry—or rather a drawn-out, terrified wail—erupted from the slope on the other side of the canyon. It was an unearthly cry, wrung from a soul catching its first glimpse of hell.

It was Brad Borrman.

Murchison and Cathy were astonished and shaken by the cry.

"That's Borrman," Longarm explained, smiling thinly at them. "I left him in the grave he was digging for you. I hit him pretty hard, but he must have just regained his senses."

Cathy recoiled at his words. Longarm looked away from her and at Murchison.

"Right now, I suggest you two check what's left of the barn and ranch house. You'll need blankets to wrap Slim in when you take him in to see Doc Fletcher."

"We'll need horses, too," said Cathy.

"I'll round them up," her father told her wearily. "You see about the blankets."

"And I'll see to Borrman," Longarm said, moving off.

There was no sign of Borrman. He was in the grave still—as dead as a doornail, completely covered over, buried alive. For a long moment Longarm stared down at the grave, trying to figure out what had happened.

Then he remembered the scream.

At once he found himself visualizing the terror Borrman must have felt the moment he awoke. He was unable to move. Darkness was all around him. The smell of fresh, damp soil hung heavy in his nostrils. That must have been when he screamed. After that came the full flood of panic as he tried desperately to free himself. Longarm imagined Borrman twisting his head violently from side to side—thrashing his body, too, in a desperate, fruitless effort to release himself.

But all this accomplished was to make him sink still deeper into the cold ground. As his struggles increased to a frenzy and his head sank deeper into the hole, the loose-packed soil must have fallen over his face and nostrils, suffocating him.

With a shudder, Longarm turned away.

Borrman had paid for what he had done to Tim Landon. He would not need to be taken back to Cody with the horribly burned Slim.

Chapter 13

The previous night, rather than proceed on into the mountains, Mary had decided to make camp beside the burned out J Bar ranch. As she well knew, these high mountain trails could be quite treacherous in the dark.

Riding up the trail into the mountains as dawn broke the next day, she had not gone far when she noticed a rider pounding down the trail toward her. Reining in her mount, she watched the rider closely. It was the former sheriff, Clint Swenson. Remembering what Smoke and Toby had told her, she realized at once that she was watching the approach of a very dangerous man.

Lifting her Winchester from its scabbard, she levered a fresh cartridge into the firing chamber and cantered forward to intercept Swenson. The big man did not slow down when he saw her cutting across his path. Indeed, she caught a malevolent grin on his face.

"Hold it there, Mr. Swenson," Mary called. "Pull up!"

He just laughed and kept riding easily toward her. Somewhat confused, Mary did not know what to do next. Should she fire upon him? Even to consider such a thing was to dismiss it.

"I'm warning you!" she cried, her voice quavering.

"And I'm warning you," Swenson said, pulling his mount to a halt beside her, his sixgun appearing in his hand as if by magic, its enormous bore aimed at her head. "Drop that rifle!"

Furious with herself, Mary did as she was told.

"Fine!" Swenson crowed. "That fellow Long is riding hard on my trail. He'll think twice now before closing with me. You are going to help me get out of this mess, Miss Mary. Now turn around and ride on ahead of me. We're heading for the Double M."

"No!" Mary said. "I will not let you use me to escape justice!"

Swenson's face went cold. The gun in his hand went off and Mary felt something hot snap past her cheek. "Do it or I'll kill you. I don't have anything to lose now, but you have everything. Now ride!"

Mary cut her horse around and started back the way she had come, seething.

• • •

172

Longarm had almost overtaken Swenson when he saw the lone rider appear out of nowhere and ride to intercept the former sheriff. At first, he could not make out who it was. Spurring his horse to a gallop, he soon narrowed the distance enough for him to be able to discern the rider's identity. To his astonishment, he saw that it was Mary. He wanted to cry out, to warn her, but he knew that at that distance she would not be able to hear him.

He bent over his horse and rowelled furiously in a desperate attempt to overtake Swenson before he confronted the girl. But Swenson was still out of Longarm's range when he fired his warning shot at Mary and then rode off with her.

What on earth Mary was doing out here, so far from Judge Kyle's office, Longarm had no idea. But he knew why Swenson had taken Mary with him. He was going to use her as a hostage while he retrieved the ransom money and then fled south. He was a desperate man and a dangerous one. Any threats he might make concerning Mary would have to be taken seriously.

Cursing his bad luck, Longarm galloped after them, content now to follow at a reasonable distance and wait for any opening that might afford itself. He already had one recourse. Murchison had given him a note to give to Red Robinson, one of his top hands, a man the cattleman was grooming for ramrod. The note instructed Red to give Longarm all the assistance he might need in bringing in Clint Swenson. At the time, Longarm had not thought the note would be necessary. But as he watched Mary and Swenson ride on past the burned-out J Bar, he knew differently.

• • •

The moment Longarm rode into the Big Outfit's compound, Murchison's ranch hands appeared from all directions, armed to the teeth, slowly closing about him. Longarm pulled up and waited. When the men were close enough, he smiled casually. "I'm looking for Red Robinson," he told them.

A tall, taciturn hand stepped out of the ring and approached his mount. "That's me, mister."

Longarm handed him the note Murchison had given him. Robinson read it quickly, then looked up at Longarm.

"This is Mr. Murchison's handwriting, I'll vouch for that. Where is he? And where is Miss Cathy?"

"They're both safe. Clint Swenson and two of his men took Cathy for ransom, but she is free now, on her way to Cody with Murchison. They have Slim Ratch with them. He has been burned pretty bad."

The trace of a pleased grin lit Robinson's face.

"The thing is," Longarm continued, "Swenson is still loose. He knows where Murchison cached the ransom money, and he's going after it. I need help to apprehend him."

Robinson swung around to face the other ranch hands. "You heard him, boys. Saddle up!"

As the men hurried back across the compound to saddle their horses, Longarm beckoned Robinson closer. "Do you know that grove of cottonwoods near a stream? It's close by a pine ridge a few miles from here."

"I know it."

"That's where Murchison cached the money, and that's where Swenson is heading right now."

"We'll get him."

"There's just one more thing," Longarm told Robinson. "It's about Judge Kyle's secretary."

"Mary?"

"Swenson has her for a hostage. We'll have to be careful."

Robinson frowned. "How in blazes did that happen?"

"It happened."

"We'll be careful," Robinson said.

"And, as the new marshal in this county, I'll be in charge of this posse. Will you tell your men that?"

"I will."

"Then lead the way."

The Big Outfit's riders rode hard to the cottonwood grove, and on Longarm's orders spread out to surround it as soon as it came into view. But they were too late. In the distance, well beyond the grove, two riders were heading south.

"Spread out!" Longarm told Red. "Surround him, but keep your weapons in your holsters."

Red nodded and passed the word.

In less than a quarter of an hour Swenson and Mary had been overtaken, even though Swenson had done all he could to pull away. His problem was Mary. As Longarm had surmised, the girl was smart enough to ride heavy, holding her horse back. Not much, but enough. And, if Swenson needed her as a hostage, he had to stay with her.

At last, seeing the last Double M rider cutting him off, he pulled up and wheeled about to face his pursuers. Then he caught sight of Longarm. Reaching over, he snatched Mary's reins from her hands, then nudged his horse to a walk toward Longarm. He was anxious to palaver, it seemed.

Longarm cut toward him. The three met well inside the circle of riders.

"Let her go, Swenson. Then we'll talk."

"Do you know how much I've got in these saddle-bags, Long? Half of it is yours if you play your cards right."

"I said let Mary go. We'll talk about that money later."

"You interested?"

"Sure, I'm interested. A lawman's always interested in stolen money."

Swenson's eyes narrowed. He was satisfied that there was no chance he could deal with Longarm. He had to try another angle. He drew his gun and pointed it at Mary across his body. Longarm's raw shoulder had made it impossible for him to match the speed of Swenson's draw, so he did nothing.

"If you shoot Mary, Swenson, these riders behind me will tear you to pieces."

"No they won't. Not if I just wound her some and promise that the next shot will finish her. They won't think I'm bluffing then."

Swenson was right. It would work. There wasn't a Double M rider behind him who wouldn't draw back to save Mary under such a threat. Longarm glanced at the girl. "Mary," he told her sharply, "dig your spurs and ride!"

She did not hesitate. As her horse shot forward, ripping the reins from Swenson's hand, Longarm flung himself at Swenson. The gun in Swenson's hand went off, but the shot went wild as Longarm struck Swenson. Swenson was able to stay in his saddle, however. Clubbing down viciously with his gun, he knocked Longarm to the ground.

As Longarm fell away, Swenson wheeled his horse and galloped toward the nearest Double M rider. The cowpoke was taken completely by surprise. Before he could draw his weapon and aim it, Swenson had shot him out of his saddle. No longer having to match Mary's speed, Swenson rowelled the powerful dun and slowly pulled away from the Double M riders. Soon they were strung out behind him as he headed back across the grassland toward the mountains.

His head as sore as his shoulder, Longarm rode hard to keep pace, Mary and Red keeping close behind him. Soon they had entered the valley where Longarm and Juan Romero had built their ranch. It was obvious what Swenson intended. Once past the J Bar and into the mountains, he would be able to give his pursuers the slip and eventually make it across the Divide to the western slopes and freedom.

It was Mary who shouted to Longarm, pointing out the lone rider. He was directly ahead of them, cutting across the flat just below the J Bar. And he was riding hard, directly at Swenson. Looking closely, Longarm saw who it was and swore softly.

"It's Murchison!" Longarm shouted to Mary.

"He'll be killed!" Mary cried. "Swenson will shoot him down."

Still riding hard, Longarm stood up in his stirrups to get a better view. Swenson and Murchison were galloping at top speed toward each other, and each had a gun gleaming in his hand.

177

Closer and closer the two men rode until it appeared they were going to collide. Swenson fired first. Murchison sagged forward slightly, then straightened and kept coming. Again Swenson fired. This time it seemed to Longarm that a puff of dust exploded on Murchison's shoulder, yet still the cattleman kept coming.

Then he too fired. Swenson flung out both arms and toppled backward off his horse. Murchison pulled up and, circling Swenson, sent round after round into the man until he emptied his revolver. Only then did he allow himself to slip slowly out of his saddle to the ground.

Longarm galloped through the encircling riders toward the fallen rancher. As he dismounted, he heard the sound of distant pounding hooves, and turned to look.

"Longarm!" Mary cried, dismounting behind him. "It's Cathy!"

But Longarm did not need to be told. As Cathy rode hard toward them, he glimpsed, far behind her, the horse she and her father had been leading, the blanketed figure of Slim Ratch folded over its saddle. The two of them had been on their way to Cody when Murchison must have caught sight of Swenson fleeing before his pursuers.

Red Robinson was down on one knee beside the wounded cattleman. Glancing up at Longarm, he shook his head. The old man was finished. Swenson was on his back a few feet away, his chest a bloody mess, half his face shot away.

Like two medieval knights, they had met on the field of battle, neither one giving quarter.

For Murchison, it had been a matter of honor.

* * *

Fresh mountain flowers had been placed in front of each cross, Longarm noted, as he and Mary rode up onto the ridge and approached the graves of Carlotta and Juan Romero. Mary pulled up and allowed Longarm to ride closer, then dismount and proceed on foot to the graves.

Uncovering his head, he came to a halt beside the crosses. He bowed his head silently. This time he was saying goodbye. It did not take long. Placing his hat back on his head, he returned to his horse, mounted, and rode back down the trail with Mary.

They heard a horse overtaking them from the slope above and pulled up. Cathy Murchison rode down through the pines and gained the trail just behind them. Longarm touched the brim of his hat to her, and Mary smiled in greeting as Cathy rode alongside.

"I figured it was you put those flowers there," Longarm said to Cathy.

"When I saw you coming I knew you'd appreciate some privacy."

"That was thoughtful of you. As a matter of fact, I had come to say goodbye."

"You're leaving?"

"Yes, I am."

The three of them started up together and rode in silence a ways. Then Cathy looked at Longarm. "Why? That J Bar land is yours now. It's a fine spread, and you have my word the Double M will leave you in peace."

"That ain't it, Cathy. I've sold the place to Mary, here. She thinks she would like to get out of that office job she has now. And for me, this country has grim, unpleasant memories I'd just as soon leave behind."

"And I promised him," Mary said, "that I would look after Carlotta and Juan's graves."

Cathy nodded somberly. "I hope you will let me join you in that."

They were riding into a clearing that overlooked the same stream that ran past the J Bar. Longarm pulled up. Mary and Cathy did also.

"You two will be going straight on down from here," Longarm told them. "I'll be cutting south, back through these mountains. It's the fastest way back to Denver for me."

"I'll ride ahead, Marshal," Cathy said. "Goodbye and good luck."

"Thank you, ma'am."

Mary waited until Cathy had disappeared around a bend in the trail. "I will see you again, won't I?" she asked.

Longarm smiled at her. "Seems to me you'll have to visit Denver soon to buy some things while the ranch is being fixed up. How would you like that?"

"I'd love it."

"And maybe whenever the smoke and grime of Denver starts to blacken my heart, I'll come north to the J Bar and we'll go pick a fresh bouquet of wild flowers."

He leaned over then and kissed Mary. It was a long kiss that told her that he did indeed want her to visit him in Denver. Then he sat back in his saddle and tipped his hat to her. She put her horse on down the trail. He sat his horse and watched her ride off.

Just before she rode out of sight, she turned in her saddle and waved. He waved back, then cut his horse south.

Look for

LONGARM AND SANTA ANNA'S GOLD

sixtieth novel in the bold
LONGARM series from Jove

available now!